Leslie's Journal

A novel by Allan Stratton

Annick Press Ltd.

Toronto • New York • Vancouver

© 2000 Allan Stratton (text)
Annick Press Ltd.

Second printing, March 2002

Edited by Barbara Pulling
Copy edited by Elizabeth McLean
Cover photograph by Lorne Bridgman/Westside Studio
Cover design by Chris Dixon
Interior design by Tanya Lloyd/Spotlight Designs
Cover model: Emily Getz
Cover calligraphy by Erin Gibbs

We acknowledge the support of the Canada Council for the Arts,
the Ontario Arts Council, and the Government of Canada through
the Book Publishing Industry Development Program (BPIDP) for
our publishing activities.

Cataloguing in Publication Data
Stratton, Allan
    Leslie's Journal

    ISBN 1-55037-665-9 (bound)   ISBN 1-55037-664-0 (pbk.)

    I. Title.
PS8587.T723L47 2000   jC813.54   C00-930790-7
PZ7.S91212Le 2000

The text in this book was typeset in Garamond and Limehouse Script.

Distributed in Canada by:
Firefly Books Ltd.
3680 Victoria Park Avenue
Willowdale, ON
M2H 3K1

Published in the U.S.A. by:
Annick Press (U.S.) Ltd.
Distributed in the U.S.A. by:
Firefly Books (U.S.) Inc.
P.O. Box 1338, Ellicott Station
Buffalo, NY 14205

Printed and bound in Canada by Friesens.
Visit us at: www.annickpress.com

Acknowledgments

The characters and situations in this book are entirely fictional. Entirely real are the many people whose input helped me write it. For their professional insight, I would like to thank Dr. Harvey Armstrong of Parents for Youth; counselor Terry Graham; lawyer Christie Milne; and Detective Inspector Tony Warr, Detective Constable Tracey Marshall and Detective John Relph of the Toronto Police Service's Behavioral Assessment Section. I would also like to thank Barbara Pulling and Rick Wilks at Annick Press; adult readers Victoria Stewart, Louise Baldaccino, Dean Cooke, Jon Pearce and Daniel Legault; and, above all, teen readers Yvonne Czerny, Norah Love, Laura Nanni and Suzanne Smith.

for my students

One

It's only the first week and already school sucks. I've got Ms. Graham again for English.

Today she said every class is going to start with fifteen minutes of journal writing, which is what we're doing now. This is supposed to train us to "reflect freely on our personal experiences." What a load. It's to give her fifteen minutes with nothing to do.

Also, since our journals will be about personal feelings, she says she won't read them. "Your journal is just for you. But write, write, write. As with everything else in this world, you'll only get out of it what you put into it." According to her, this is a "Life Lesson." But what it *really* is is an excuse for her to get out of marking.

A year of journals! Can I scream yet? It's so boring I keep forgetting to breathe. And each day when it's over—talk about an insult—she says she's going to collect them and lock them up in her filing cabinet. Yeah, that's right, they're going in her filing cabinet, like we're a bunch of babies who'll lose them or something.

But okay. Journals beat having her teach. Last year, she either read aloud to us or we read aloud to her, then she'd stop and ask us stupid questions about what we'd just heard. This last part was really hilarious, because nobody ever gave her an answer. We all just stared up at her like we were dead and watched her eyes go funny. No kidding, her eyes were amazing. Like gerbils. They darted around desperate for a hand to pop into the air while the silence kept getting worse and worse until she couldn't stand it any more and she'd blurt out the answer herself.

Normal teachers would figure if students are passed out then maybe they should do something. LIKE, HELLO, MAYBE STOP ASKING SUCH DUMB QUESTIONS! But not Ms. Graham. She just went from dumb to dumber, getting more and more squirrelly. She'd be sweating, and there'd be red patches on her neck and she'd be wiping the sweat off her hands onto her dress...It was disgusting.

That's when she'd tell us to read the next chapter silently and answer the questions on some handouts she'd pass around for homework. Which of course we never did. We just pretended we hadn't heard her and that the handouts didn't exist. At the end of class, we'd crumple them into balls and toss them in the general direction of the wastebasket. It's like, whole rain forests got clearcut so Ms. Graham could stuff her filing cabinet with handouts that all ended up in the garbage.

Then, pretty soon, we pretended Ms. Graham didn't exist either. We'd just come in, put our heads on our desks and go to sleep. Which was fine by her, I guess, because at least if we were sleeping we weren't throwing chalk. Or handouts.

It was soooo painful.

Near the end of the year, she went Missing in Action. They said she was away with chronic bronchitis, but we figured she was having a breakdown. Over the summer the story went around that she'd knocked over a shelf of light fixtures at Wal-Mart and ended up under a pile of lamp-shades babbling hysterically while trying to choke herself to death with an electric cord until the ambulance came and hauled her off in a straitjacket.

Well, that's the rumor. And even if it isn't true, it should be, because obviously she's back for more and she's nutty as ever. Right now she's floating around with this vague look, smelling kind of stale in a pale gray billowy thing. She looks like a human dustball. Wait. She's just come to rest in front of the window. She's looking out. I wonder if she's thinking of jumping.

It's kind of sad, really. I mean, if she wasn't a teacher, I'd feel sorry for her. Once upon a time she was somebody's baby, playing patty-cakes and having everybody kissing her and saying she was a cutie. Then she grew up. I picture her all alone in some tiny apartment, surrounded by cats and stacks of unmarked assignments, praying that tomor-row will be better. And it never is.

Poor Ms. Graham. It's not like she *wants* to be boring. That's why I almost feel guilty when we all torture her. Who we *should* torture — *really, really* torture, with hot coals and a pair of hedge clippers — is Ernie Boulder. He has short greasy hair, cystic acne and a squishy tongue he likes to stick in girls' ears for a joke. He also has a dent in his forehead from where somebody hit him with a shovel when he was little. Too bad they didn't hit harder.

Ernie is the grossest pig in the school, and in this school there's a lot of competition. He has only one redeeming feature. If you want to lose weight, just think about making out with him. You won't be able to eat for a week.

Anyway, Ernie The Pus-head Boulder worked it so he sits one seat ahead of me in three separate classes. What's worse, he apparently thinks it is majorly funny to stick a couple of pencils up his nose and pretend to be a walrus. The real reason he does this is to have an excuse to let his pencils fall on the floor so he can bend down to pick them up and look up my skirt while he's at it.

Today I got my revenge. I waited till lunch, when I knew he'd be in the cafeteria with lots of people all around. Then I marched right up to his table and said in a big loud voice, "Look Pus-head, you cop a look between my legs one more time and I'll personally pop your zits with a compass!"

There was this roar of laughter, hooting and foot-stomping. Ernie was so embarrassed, I thought his cysts would explode. As for me, I just snapped my fingers and diva-ed my way to the parking lot for a smoke.

That's where I met the vice-principal, Mr. Carrouthers, out on a little narc duty. "I want to see you in my office, young lady."

Sorry, journal, according to Ms. Graham it's time for

you to go into the filing cabinet. Tomorrow, I'll tell you what happened with the Nazi.

P.S. Dear Ms. Graham: You promised our journals were going to be private. So in case you're secretly reading this to get some cheap thrills, you are nothing but a crazy perverted liar, and it's not my fault if it sends you over the edge.

Two

Vice-principals are basically school cops. They like to act tough and eat donuts. So, all things considered, I guess Mr. Carrouthers is in the right job. They say that once upon a time he used to be a phys. ed. teacher. Now the only thing he gets to exercise is his voice. As a result, he's turned into this elephant in a suit.

It's pathetic, really. He walks around all tough and important, like he's the FBI or something, when all he really is is some old high-school teacher who gets his kicks yelling at teenagers. I mean, he spends his whole life sneaking behind cars in the school parking lot to catch smokers, or smelling kids' breath for alcohol or pot, or going around with a flashlight at school dances to make sure nobody's having sex on the football field or under the stairwells. What kind of sickie would get off on that?

Last year, in grade nine, Mr. Carrouthers was always hauling me down to his office. I practically lived there. I used to joke he kept wanting to see me because he had the hots for me (yuck, gross), but really it was on account of me being late and skipping all the time. My parents had just started what they called a "trial separation" and I wasn't taking it so well.

I'm still not. Especially since Mom went from being still-married-sort-of to being an officially designated Single Mother. Now whenever she sees politicians on TV going on about single moms she starts to cry. Then she yells at me. It's like she's afraid if she doesn't crack down I'm going to turn into this demon seed from a broken home, end up on some talk show maybe. "You're going to improve your behavior," she yells. "Do you hear me, Leslie?"

"No. I'm deaf."

"Cut the attitude!"

I give her the look. She goes ballistic. "Don't give me that look."

"Then stop yelling at me. It's not my fault Dad found someone better. Keep it up and I'll leave too."

That's when her face goes white and she rocks on her feet like I punched her or something. Then she runs to her room and closes the door and makes these strange animal sounds. And I want to die. I don't want to hurt her. Really. I just don't want her to yell at me all the time. Why does everything have to be my fault?

Last year after Dad left was pretty bad. I couldn't be

around anybody. Sometimes I took off to the mall to see how many movies I could sneak into at the cineplex, or to watch music videos on the wall of big-screen TVs at Laserama Electronics, or to panhandle beside the bank machine to see if I could make a living if I ever had to run away from home. But mostly, I just hung out in the far cubicle of the girls' washroom on the second floor east wing and cried.

Needless to say, whenever I did show up for class there was a note telling me to report to the vice-principal. In fact, me getting hauled down to the office turned into what my drama teacher would call a "Ritual."

At first Mr. Carrouthers tried to smarten me up by giving me after-school detentions. No way for that. So guess what he'd do when I'd skip detentions? Give me two-day suspensions. Is that funny or what? I skip school and my punishment is that I get to skip *more* school. Mr. Carrouthers is a genius in the Stupid Department.

Which brings me back to getting caught in the parking lot. It turns out Brainiac hadn't seen my cigarette after all. Instead, he wanted to talk to me about my "inappropriate dress."

"It's not inappropriate," I say when we're in his office. "It's retro." What it really is is a black vinyl micro-mini with fishnets, platforms and a crop top. Since last May I'm happy to say I haven't needed padding.

"You know what I'm getting at," Mr. Carrouthers snaps back, all eyebrows.

"I'm afraid I don't," I smile sweetly. "Perhaps you'd like to explain it to me." (Teachers hate that smile, because they know exactly what I'm thinking but they can't do anything.)

Mr. Carrouthers decides to put me in my place. He gives me his famous silent routine. It's deadly. He stares down at a person without any expression, like they're a bug or something, and he just keeps staring. Finally the person goes crazy and starts to twitch. That's when he has them.

Well, he doesn't have *me*. Last year, maybe, when I was just a niner who thought getting sent to the office meant something. But I've been called down so much by now I'm inoculated. Instead of getting scared, I look him straight in the eye. "Mr. Carrouthers," I ask, "are you saying I look like a slut?"

"That's not what I said," he chokes.

"But it's what you meant, isn't it? Unfortunately, I'm only a junior. I don't know anything about sluts. Perhaps you could tell me about them. For instance, how exactly *do* sluts dress?" (And here I give him an even sweeter smile.) "In your experience."

We stare at each other, hard, him really trying to break me down, me keeping cool by counting his nose hairs. Mr. Carrouthers has hair growing out of his nose and his ears and all over the back of his hands and fingers. For a second I picture him naked. I nearly barf.

Suddenly, for a split second, he looks away. I win. "You

will go home, change and report back to this office when you're decent," he mutters. "That will be all."

Go home? I don't think so. I have some baggy clothes in my locker I can put on. They're what I leave the apartment in, otherwise Mom wouldn't let me out the door. I wear them over top, take them off as soon as I get in the elevator and stuff them in a plastic bag. It sounds dumb, but it saves a fight, and we fight enough as it is.

I tilt my head, smile at Mr. Carrouthers, get up and roll my eyes. "Have a nice day," I say.

I step out into the main office, and there's this senior lounging on the counter waiting for a secretary. I walk towards the hall staring straight ahead, but I can tell his eyes are following me. Not just following me—they're burning into the back of my head.

At the doorway, I stop and turn. "What's your damage?"

I expect him to go all red. But he just grins, winks and keeps staring. So I give him the finger, toss my hair and make an exit.

What a jerk!

Three

Katie was shocked when I told her what I said to Mr. Carrouthers.

Katie is always shocked. That's one of the things I like best about her. Whenever I'm bored, I go up to her and say, "Hey, Katie, guess what I just did?" and before I have a chance to say a word her eyes are so wide they look like they're going to fall out of her head.

Katie's been my best friend since I moved to this pit six years ago because of Dad getting transferred. I arrived in October. Everyone was already into their little cliques, and when I was introduced to the class it was like somebody'd just farted.

At recess, no one would talk to me. All the boys wanted to do was run around like a bunch of morons screaming their heads off. But the girls—they were just plain mean. They were all in groups acting cute and when I'd come over they'd turn their backs on me and start to whisper and laugh. Mom had made me wear this brand-new outfit with a sweater vest. Nobody else was wearing sweater vests, though, because apparently the Fashion Police had decided they were against the law or something.

Anyway, there I was, feeling like a giant dog turd. I knew I couldn't cry—that would be *too* embarrassing. So instead I acted like I had something very important to do and marched off the asphalt to the fence at the back of the school yard.

There was a girl there with big cheeks and glasses, sitting under a tree, reading a Nancy Drew book. She looked pretty normal, except she was moving her lips. So I sat down about twenty feet from her and pretended to stare at this anthill, like I was a member of the junior science club or something. What I was really doing was praying my dad would get fired so we could move back home where I at least had a few friends. (I can hardly remember their names any more, except for Annie Wilson, who stopped writing me after three measly letters—and after she swore on her cat Pooky's grave that we'd be friends to eternity.)

I was just about to lose it when I heard a voice. "Oh, hi. You're Leslie, right?" I looked over and it was Moving-Lip Girl. "I'm sorry for being so rude," she went on. "It's just that Nancy's gone to the haunted well all alone in the middle of the night and I didn't even see you come over."

I shrugged as if I didn't care one way or the other.

"My name's Katie. I sit three rows over from you. Where are you from?"

"Seattle."

"Seattle? But that's in the United States!" Her eyes went all big like this was the most amazing thing she'd ever heard, and we've been inseparable ever since.

I love Katie. I couldn't have made it through last year without her. During the stuff with my parents—the yelling, the fights, the separation—she was always ready to listen or to make me laugh. Even when her mother told her to get off the phone, I knew she'd find a way to call back within ten minutes. And for Katie, calling back after getting the Word was a really big deal.

Katie is what adults call "well behaved"—which they apparently think is a compliment. Personally, I call "well behaved" being a suck, and it is the one thing about Katie that sometimes bugs me. Luckily, Katie *knows* she's a suck.

"I just can't help myself," she laughs, eyes bulging. So how can I stay mad? I mean, that's exactly what I say, only for the opposite reason.

I guess that's why we're friends: we can forgive each other. Katie says that when she looks at me she sees a terrific person who really wants to do good. I tease that when I look at her I see a spawn of Satan who really wants to cut loose. Only I'm not totally teasing. The reason Katie loves to be shocked by my stories is because I do and say the stuff she can't.

Katie's biggest problem is her mother. Mrs. Kincaid is this giant spider sucking the life out of her. She's this giant slug oozing slime. She's this—don't get me started!

Let's just say that Mrs. Kincaid thinks everyone and everything should be nice. As in "Don't you look *nice!*" Or lovely. As in "Don't you look *lovely!*" Or just about perfect. As in "Don't you look *just about perfect!*" (Not *perfect,* mind you. *Just about* perfect. That's because she thinks the only perfect one is her.) Naturally, Mrs. Kincaid doesn't think I'm nice or lovely or anywhere close to being just about perfect. What Mrs. Kincaid thinks I am is trouble. As in "Leslie Phillips is nothing but *trouble.*" That's what I heard her say to Mr. Kincaid one night last year when she thought me and Katie were down in the rec room watching TV.

At first I was hurt. I'd always thought she liked me. But obviously things had changed since my parents' separation and the move into our dump of an apartment and me starting to go wild. "Acting out" is how our family counselor put it when I got caught sneaking home drunk. To hear my mom tell it, you'd have thought I was an alcoholic or something.

"But you're only in grade nine!"

"Yeah, well, I'm fourteen, so get used to it."

That's when the counselor said I was "acting out." "How would you know?" I yelled. "You're just some old turkey. Get stuffed, why don't you?" I never went back to see him again.

Anyway, I decided I didn't have to care what Mrs. Kincaid thought. After all, I was Katie's friend, not hers. At least that's what I figured until Katie phoned last year at the end of spring break and said we had to talk.

"But we always talk," I said. "We're talking right now."

"This is different. We have to talk in private."

"Well, this is private. Unless your mother's listening in again. Hello, Mrs. Kincaid, isn't it a *lovely* day out? Why, I'd say it's *just about perfect.*"

"Cut it out, Leslie. I'm serious. We really have to talk. In person."

My heart started thumping because Katie was sounding so weird. I imagined maybe she had some kind of terrible disease or her parents had been killed in a car crash. We decided to meet at two o'clock at my place, because my mom would be out doing groceries. After we hung up, I just sat there shaking, thinking of how I'd have to act brave and comfort her.

But when Katie arrived she didn't look sick or anything. Just sort of fidgety. And she smiled a lot, really fake, and said, no, she was fine and her parents were fine and wasn't spring break great and they should give a prize to whoever invented it.

"Cut the crap, Katie," I said. "I've been worried sick all day. What's the deal with this Having to Talk? In Person. In Private."

"Well..." She took a deep breath and started scrunching her knees and staring at the coffee table. "My mom..."

"Yeah? Your mom what?"

"My mom thinks we shouldn't spend so much time together."

My stomach went hollow. "Why? Is she afraid we're turning into lesbians or something?"

"No."

"Well, so what if we were? Your mom is a bigot."

"No, she isn't."

"Yes, she is." I gulped for air. "She hates me."

"She says we should expand our circle of friends."

"Yeah, right. That's just a nice way of saying, 'I think you should stop seeing Leslie.'"

"It is not."

"Besides, I don't want to 'expand my circle of friends.' I want things the way they are."

Katie started flapping her hands and looking at me all helpless like she always does when her mom means business.

"It's not fair. First Dad runs out on me. And now you."

"I'm not running out on you."

"You are so."

Suddenly I couldn't take it any more and I started to blubber. Without even thinking, Katie gave me a big hug and I hugged her back, and we didn't let go. When I settled down, she took my head in both hands and stared deep into my eyes. "Leslie," she said, "you're my best friend in the whole world. And you'll always be my best friend. Cross my heart."

Her eyes were so serious and sweet I wanted to cry all over again. But instead I started to giggle. And then Katie started to giggle too. Before we knew it, we were both rolling around laughing and everything seemed okay again.

But Mrs. Kincaid was serious. (Never trust a mother who smells like hair spray.) Our first day back after the spring break, Mrs. Kincaid had Katie hand out invitations to a slumber party. Of course I got one too—Mrs. Kincaid was too smart to make Katie take me off the list. But it was all part of her master plan. Because instead of Katie and me doing something fun on our own, we'd be with a bunch of other girls. Other girls who hate me and make me feel left out.

Head of the Leaving-Me-Out Department is Ashley Walker. She goes to Katie's church, and ever since that first slumber party she's butted into our friendship. She makes Katie feel guilty if she doesn't participate in their stupid church youth group activities. So instead of doing stuff on the weekend with me, half the time Katie ends up being Ashley's buddy selling youth charity raffle tickets or doing some youth charity car wash or attending a geeky youth weiner roast.

Katie even made me come and hear her and Ashley the first time they performed in the church's junior choir. I almost puked watching Ashley flounce around in her polyester choir robe, like she was a big deal or something.

Last summer was worst of all. Ashley got Katie to go with her to the church youth leadership training camp, so for two whole weeks I was stuck on my own. "You could have come," Katie said. "The youth group's always looking for new members."

Yeah, right. New members who are nice and lovely and just about perfect.

God, I hate Ashley. I told Katie, but she said I shouldn't be mean because Ashley has problems too.

"Like what?"

"Dermatitis."

"Dermatitis?" I laughed. "You mean she's all scaly."

"Leslie, don't make me choose sides."

"Is that a warning?"

"Just don't." Katie turned on her heel and walked off. I felt lost. She never used to get mad at me. What had I done to deserve it?

Life doesn't make sense. It's against the law for somebody to try and steal your bike, yet apparently it doesn't matter if somebody tries to steal your best friend. Well, you can always get a new bike. But how do you replace a best friend?

Four

Today is Friday. At lunch I go into the cafeteria, and I see Katie and Ashley A-hole with a bunch of other girls in a clump by the window. Katie and I used to have lunch alone, only now her table has turned into Girl Central. They're always in a group, pointing and whispering and generally being embarrassing. At the moment, they're looking out at the track.

"So what's the big deal?" I say.

"Leslie, look. By the goalposts," squeals Katie. "He's just transferred and his name is Jason McCready and he's a senior and he has a motorcycle and ohmigod!" She sighs and does this fake fainting routine like I'm supposed to be impressed she's got hormones.

When I look out, I see it's him, the guy from the office. And come to think of it, he *is* pretty cute, slouched all alone against the goalpost, one knee slightly bent, hands in his back pockets, head back to catch some rays. He looks like an underwear model with clothes on.

Naturally I play it cool. "Oh, him," I say, stuffing my face with tuna sandwich. "We've already met."

"No way."

"Not my type," I yawn, and I turn away like he's the last thing on my mind.

"Liar," Ashley sneers. "I'll bet you've never even seen him before."

"Oh, no? Well, I've not only seen him before, I've given him the finger."

Katie gasps. "What did he do?" Her eyes are like pies.

"Nothing. He just smiled."

Katie is in awe. "Smiled? You mean he likes you?"

The idea hadn't crossed my mind, but I'm not going to say no and look stupid in front of Ashley. So instead, I check my nails. "Some of us have what it takes."

"Liar," Ashley snaps again. "If you and Jason are such good friends, let's see you go out and talk to him. He'll tell you to get lost."

I'm trapped. But I'm not going to let Ashley show me up.

"Candy from a baby," I laugh, and I head out to the track, praying by the time I get there he'll be gone.

He isn't. When I get within ten feet of him, I slow down. I stop. I can tell he knows someone's there, but he keeps his eyes closed and lets the breeze play through his curly brown hair. His shirt's hanging out and open, and under it he's got on this incredibly tight T-shirt. Can I breathe?

I can feel the girls staring at me. There's no turning back. "Hi. You must be Jason."

A pause. "If you say so." His eyes are still closed.

"We, uh, we met in the office."

He opens his eyes. They are so blue. "Oh. So you must be the principal."

For a second, I don't get it. "Uh . . ." I want to run. I want to cry. But I'm frozen.

"Are those your friends?" He nods towards the cafeteria.

The girls have their faces squashed against the window like they're in kindergarten. They look demento, especially Katie, who is waving her hand so fast I'm surprised it doesn't fall off.

"Friends? I've never seen them before."

He smiles. His teeth are very white. "Come here."

I take two baby steps, then toss my head and walk right up to him. All of a sudden, he puts his arm around me and gives me a kiss. And not just any kiss. He actually slips me the tongue!

He smiles again. "Gotta fly," he says.

"Okay," I say back. I feel sort of absent-minded, like an amnesia patient on some Movie of the Week. My knees are wobbly. I try not to fall down.

"By the way, my name is Leslie," I call after him.

"Right," he says. He waves, real casual and slow, and keeps on walking. I turn to the cafeteria window and curtsy. Katie's eyes are right out of their sockets. Ashley looks as if she's just had a heart attack.

And me? I'm in love!

Five

After school on Friday, I found out where his locker is. On the first floor in the south wing. Number 1124. Just my luck. It's miles away.

Spying on a guy's locker is tricky, because if he finds out, for sure he'll never want to see you again. But this morning I couldn't stop myself. All weekend I kept thinking that if I wasn't there first thing when Jason got to school, he'd meet some other girl and it'd be all over.

I tried to blend into the walls, walking really slowly up and down the corridor, pretending to read *To Kill a Mockingbird,* and then stopping for some water at the drinking fountain. Was that dumb or what? I looked like a browner and I had to pee all morning.

To make matters worse, Jason didn't show up. He doesn't even seem to be in school today. Maybe he's had an accident. Maybe he's in the hospital. Maybe he's dying. Maybe he's switched schools. Or maybe I'm just being stupid. Which is probably more like it. I bet he's just skipping, which is what I'd be doing if I wasn't trying so hard to see him.

Jason, Jason, Jason. Love is a killer, especially if you can't talk to anyone about it. Like, if I tell Katie how I feel, she'll tell Ashley and Ashley'll tell the world. As for Mom? Get real. When I'm suicidal she laughs it off as a "phase," and when I'm happy she gets suspicious.

I'm extra obsessed on account of I was looking forward to seeing Jason after my crummy weekend. It was Dad's turn to have me, only he was busy Saturday. Fine. He's *always* busy Saturday, working overtime, he says, since Mom is out to nail him in the divorce. (Which she says is a dirty lie, but that's another story.)

To cut it short, Dad picks me up Sunday at about two o'clock and tells me today is going to be really special—he has a surprise for me at his apartment. As we drive out to Oakville, I'm thinking, "Great, he's finally fixed his VCR so we can watch movies instead of being stuck staring at each other over buckets of cold Chinese takeout."

Well, the VCR isn't the surprise. When he opens the door, I see a couple of empty packing boxes in the hallway, and there's this strange smell of air freshener. Then Dad calls out, "We're home," and all of a sudden SHE bounces in from the bedroom looking like a Colgate commercial.

Her name is Brenda. I know that without anyone saying, because Mom and Dad used to fight about her all the time before they split up. And now I get to see her, all cute and perky, this overgrown cheerleader out to make a good impression. "Hi," she says, and out comes her hand like she actually expects me to shake it.

"This is the surprise?" I glare at Dad.

Brenda ignores what I think is a pretty obvious signal. "You must be Leslie," she beams.

"And you must be the Bitch," I reply.

Brenda looks like someone just slapped her—if only!—and Dad's ears go red. As per usual, he knows he should say something but can't figure out what. All he can manage is a blustery, "Leslie . . ."

"No, Dave, it's all right." Brenda pats his arm. "I understand."

Dad settles down and tries his fatherly bit. "Leslie, Brenda's accepted my invitation to move in."

I look at the boxes. I sniff the air. "No kidding."

And now Dad puts his arm around her. My stomach's dissolving.

As for Brenda, she's from another planet. "I'd like to be your friend," she bubbles.

I want to explode, but I don't. Instead, I pin her with my eyes, smile and say in a sweet little voice: "Is that so? Well, if you'd like to be my friend, perhaps you could tell me why you broke up my family and ruined my life?"

"Leslie! You will apologize!" Dad shouts.

"Eat shit!"

Dad looks at Brenda like a deer caught in the headlights. "I'm sorry. I should have told her in the car." The car? He should have told me in the car? Is this my father?

"Take me home! Now!"

I look out the window the whole way back. I don't say a word. All those Saturdays he was so busy with "overtime." What a joke.

Dad stops outside my apartment building. As I open the car door, I hear him clear his throat. Here it comes.

"I'm very disappointed in you, Leslie."

"Is that a fact."

"You embarrassed me. And you embarrassed yourself."

"Whatever." I get out of the car and head up the walk.

"Come back here, young lady! I'm not finished!"

"Oh yes, you are," I think and keep going, running as

fast as I can. I get to the elevator, shoot upstairs. No way he'll follow me. He doesn't have the guts.

"Back so early?" Mom asks. She tries to act casual, but I know she's happy. She's always happy when I come back early. It means I'm mad at Dad. Well, I'm mad at her too. I slam my door, hurl myself on the bed and sob.

There's a little knock. "Honey?"

"Go away."

"What's wrong?"

"Nothing."

"That crying doesn't sound like nothing."

"Just leave me alone."

Leave me alone. That's not asking too much, is it? But does she? No! She opens the door! She starts to come in!

"Honey—"

"I...SAID...LEAVE...ME...ALONE!!!" And I throw my hairbrush at her. Why does she have to make everything so hard?

I hate this life.

And then I think of Jason. Beautiful, beautiful Jason with his deep blue eyes and curly brown hair. I picture us gunning down some deserted highway on his motorcycle, me holding on tight around his waist.

Who am I kidding? I'm in love with some guy who probably doesn't even remember I exist.

Six

It's only been a week since we started doing journals, but already a lot of the class has stopped writing. They say they wrote down everything about their life on day one. "But every day is a new adventure!" Ms. Graham exclaimed. Hello? Has she looked in the mirror lately?

Anyway, for people with no ideas, she's agreed to post a daily "Topic for Reflection." Today's topic is "What Makes Dreams Come True?" General groan, 'cause guess what? They don't. And when they do, you wish they hadn't. Take Ms. Graham. If she ever dreamed of being a teacher, I'll bet she's been kicking herself all the way to her shrink's ever since. And if she dreamed of being anything else, well, I rest my case.

All the same, lame or not, I'm going to write about it, just to stop thinking about you-know-who for two seconds. I mean my whole *life* is thinking about him, which is totally stupid and driving me crazy, but I can't help it. I pretend he's moved to Australia, only right away I imagine him in tight shorts and a cowboy hat hopping around on a kangaroo. Or I pretend he's dead, only I imagine him in his coffin, all beautiful like he's sleeping, and smelling of lilies. I picture myself kissing a rose and putting it over his heart, so that a little part of me will be with him forever. Sick or what?

Back to the topic. I only know three people who believe in dreams coming true: Mom, Katie and Walt Disney.

Mom says dreams have a catch, though. She says they only come true if you plan ahead and work hard to make them happen. This is why I'm supposed to buckle down and study, so that later on, when "opportunity knocks," I'll be able to answer the door. Not that planning ahead and working hard has done anything for her, other than getting her a divorce, a lousy apartment and temp work. When I remind her of this, she tells me to stop being negative. She says I'm too young to be cynical. I say she's too old not to be.

"But, honey, these are the best years of your life."

"Then shoot me."

This gets her all teary. "Leslie, when you say things like that, I don't know whether to laugh or cry."

So now I'm supposed to feel guilty and take it all back. No way. "If you're thinking of crying, don't."

Mom apparently believes in the Magical Land of Happy Teenagers where nobody worries about zits, or periods, or exams, or pregnancy, or AIDS, or gangs, or the future, and the most serious thing in life is a pillow fight at some slumber party. In the Magical Land of Happy Teenagers there is no sex or booze or drugs, and everyone is polite and helpful and smiles like an idiot.

Mom should be committed.

Katie also believes in dreams coming true. According to her, you don't have to work for your dreams, you just have to pray for them. According to her, God answers her prayers all the time.

"Oh yeah?" I say. "Well, He didn't give you that A you wanted in geography."

"Only because I didn't pray hard enough. But He gave me a C, and if I hadn't prayed at all I would have failed."

Katie also believes in God answering prayers because of her teeth. Since forever, she'd been praying for Him to fix her overbite. Finally, at the end of grade eight, her parents took her to an orthodontist who gave her braces. She showed me this miracle the next morning before school.

"Katie," I said, "are you trying to tell me God is a dentist?"

That made her really cross. She said if God was going to answer her prayers, it was mean for me to get picky about how He did it. In fact, it was a sin. I started to say something smart, but she just put her hands over her ears and started to hum.

"Look, Katie, I believe in God," I yelled, since it was the only thing I figured would shut her up. "I just think He's got more on His mind than your stupid braces. Making sure the planets don't collide, for one thing."

And suddenly, in the middle of the playground, I had a flash of God as some kind of Cosmic Juggler, and us as billions and trillions of balls He's got in the air. Some of us stay up and some of us fall down. And who stays up and who falls down—well, it all depends on whether He loses His concentration.

Katie liked my theory, except she said God never loses His concentration because He's perfect. She says that everything has a reason, and that God has a Divine Plan for each and every ball. If a ball falls, it's either because it didn't go where it was supposed to go, or because God planned for it to fall all along.

Katie's idea of a Divine Plan is what English teachers like Ms. Graham call Destiny. Or Fate. It's why young lovers get together at the end of a story, unless they're in *Romeo and Juliet* or *Titanic,* in which case they die.

Mom and Katie are lucky. They really believe there's a reason for everything, and that sooner or later you'll be happy if you just work or pray hard enough. I wish I could be like them, but lately I've been overcome by this fear. I just start sweating and I think—what if there isn't a plan? What if Destiny is just a fancy word for luck? I mean, what if things just happen because they happen? For no reason at all?

For example, maybe you want a Dairy Queen. Well, maybe you get one or maybe you don't—or maybe you get one, but when you step off the curb to go home you get hit by a truck. For no reason! It just happens! Or maybe you want a baby. Maybe you get one, but then maybe it grows up to be a serial killer. For no reason! It just happens!

If things just happen because they happen, then you have no control. You're helpless. We all are. Even parents. There's no one—nothing—to protect us. Not ever.

I don't want that. I want a world that makes sense. Where things have meaning. That's why even though I think Mom and Katie are crazy, I really hope they're right. Because then I can stop worrying. If my dream of Jason and me being together is part of some Divine Plan—like, if it's destined or something—then it'll just happen. Or, if dreams need a little work, I can keep checking his locker. Or, if prayer helps...Well, okay, not that I believe in it or anything, but just in case, *Dear God: If Jason comes up and asks me for a date, I promise to believe in You.*

Boy, am I ever glad no one's reading this.

Seven

God exists! I have been rescued from hell! Okay. First the hell part. Yesterday Katie invited me to another of her Saturday night slumber parties. I was kind of glad to be invited, because if I hadn't been, I'd be suicidal. But I'm also thinking, hey, we're in grade ten now—aren't we a little old for slumber parties? I mean, couldn't she at least call them sleepovers? But no, at Katie's house they really *are* slumber parties, because her mom is always home, which means no cigarettes or booze or boys. Once, as a joke, I asked Katie if I could bring some homemade hash brownies to liven things up. You should have seen her face. It was like I'd invited her to join a Satanic cult.

At Katie's slumber parties, we all sit around in the rec room in our nighties. (Except for me. I usually sleep in my underwear, so Mrs. Kincaid makes me wear an old pair of Katie's pajamas, plastered with kittens or ballerinas. Basically I look like a dork, but that's okay so long as no one takes pictures.) We eat popcorn and chips and play cards and gossip, blah blah blah. Then Mrs. Kincaid comes down with more so-called treats, like Rice Krispie squares and Jell-o fruit cup (whee!), and also stuff she makes from recipes on the back of packages, like multicolored mini-marshmallows and canned Mandarin orange slices in sour cream (help!).

I swear she's got her ear to the air vent the whole night, because the second we bring up the subject of boys she's down again to interrupt with the nutty idea that we might like to dye our hair. She hands out these Krazy Kolors that wash out—Krazy Kolors, crazy if you're a clown, maybe—and, bingo, we're all dyeing our hair and giving each other facials and rolling around in hysterics. Ha ha, remind me to laugh. Oh, and did I mention the fashion show? The thrills never stop.

It's not that I don't like facials and fashion shows. Katie and me used to have them all the time. But it was just the two of us. It's different when you do something with a friend than with a bunch of people who are just putting up with you.

Hearing the hilarity, Mrs. Kincaid comes back and whispers loud in Katie's ear, "Your father's trying to get some work done. How be you girls settle down and watch a video?" Katie always acts as if this is a great idea and puts on some sucky piece of junk they taped off the Family Channel.

After gagging for five minutes, I say something like, "Hey, let's turn down the sound and make up fake dialogue."

And Ashley either goes, "Leslie, we're enjoying this. If you aren't, why don't you go home?" or "Come on, Leslie, you're looking for an excuse to say something gross and spoil everything." When I turn to Katie for support she just flaps her hands and looks helpless. I know she doesn't want to choose sides, but her not saying anything sure feels like a choice to me.

I go off in a corner and pretend to read an old copy of *Teen People*. (*Teen People*. What a weird concept. Tell it to adults sometime.) I sigh a lot and moan and generally bug everybody until they start throwing cushions at me. Then finally it's midnight, and Mrs. Kincaid comes back down and turns the lights out.

"Sleep tight."

Argh! It is always the same and it is always torture!

So when Katie invites me this time I say, "Sure, great," but I'm seriously thinking up excuses to cancel. Until I get home, that is, and find Mom rummaging around my room in Amazon Warrior mode. It seems Mr. Carrouthers has called about my "continued inappropriate dress," and Mom has discovered I'm not wearing what I leave the house in. In fact, I'm wearing clothes she didn't even know I had.

"You're quite a piece of work, Leslie," she fumes, pointing at my secret wardrobe. She's started to dig clothes out of supposedly empty drawers under my bed, and she's throwing them onto a big pile in the middle of the room. "Tell me, what is the meaning of this?"

How am I supposed to answer? I don't even try. Instead, I point at the "Leslie's Room: Keep Out" sign on the door. "Can't you read?" I yell. "Like, whatever happened to trust?"

Mom starts shoving the pile into a green garbage bag. "These are going out with the trash."

"Just who the hell do you think you are?"

She ignores me, holding up a black bustier. "Where did you pick up this filth?"

"For your information, that filth just so happens to be presents. From Dad." This is partly true, because I bought most of this stuff with money he gave me for Christmas and my birthday. Also with money I borrowed from his wallet. (I don't call it stealing, I call it getting even. He says he gives me money instead of gifts so I can get something I'll really like. Bullshit. He'd rather spend time with precious Brenda than shop for his daughter.)

Anyway, Mom is apparently deaf. She stuffs the last of the pile into the bag and heads towards the door. "Get out of my way."

"You toss my stuff, next time you're out I'll toss your stuff!"

Mom stops in her tracks. She's so mad I think she's going to have a stroke. "You are sooo grounded!"

"Go ahead. Ground me," I glare back. "If I have to stay home, I'll make your life hell. You up for it?"

For a second, Mom gets this scared look in her eye. She knows she can't back down. But she knows I won't back down either. Stalemate. That's when I play my ace. I tell her about Katie's slumber party and how Katie was planning to introduce me to some girls from her church youth group. That cools Mom right down, seeing as she thinks Katie is such a good influence. "Will her mother be there?"

"What do you think?"

She checks anyway, calling Mrs. Kincaid that very second. To cut a long story short, I'm no longer grounded and the bag of clothes stayed in my room. I should be a diplomat or something.

Which brings me to how there's a God after all.

I'm at my locker this morning, when all of a sudden I realize I'm being stared at. I turn around, and it's Jason. He doesn't say much. He just smiles and points his finger at me. "I'll be at Mister Pizza's at 12:10." Then he winks, swivels slowly and saunters down the hall.

Katie, Ashley, Kimberly and Sara all stand there dumbstruck, their jaws bouncing off the floor. I take off fast so they won't see I feel the same way.

The rest of the morning I spend in the washroom getting ready for our date. I make sure I'm at Mister Pizza's early. But no sooner am I getting comfortable than in waltzes the coven. They sit down at the next booth.

"What are you trying to do, scare him off?" I say.

"You don't own this place," Ashley smirks.

I want to smack her, but then I see Jason crossing the road, so I let out a major sigh and move to the booth at the far end. In he walks all breezy and confident, gives me a nod, goes up to the counter and orders two slices of double cheese, pepperoni and mushrooms and a couple of Cokes. (He knows what I want without even asking—is he amazing or what?) Then he brings them to the table, passing by my so-called friends like they don't exist.

After a little small talk, Jason asks if I'm doing anything Saturday night. I tell him I'll have to check my calendar, but it's like he knows there's nothing to check. He laughs and says great, he'll pick me up at six for a quick bite and an early flick, and then we can go to this rave he knows about.

"Sure," I say. All of a sudden I remember he can't come to my place because I'm supposed to be at Katie's, so I tell him I'll be hanging out at the Southside Mall all afternoon. We arrange to meet at six at Taco Bell. Then he knocks back the rest of his Coke, says, "Catch ya later," and heads out the door.

I get up slow, stretch and glide over to the loser booth. "Guess who's going to a rave with Jason McCready Saturday night?" I gloat.

"But what about my slumber party?" Katie asks.

"Sorry," I say. "Divine intervention."

Katie looks like somebody let the air out of her balloon.

"That's okay," sniffs Ashley. "I guess we know who your *real* friends are, don't we, Katie?"

I glare at her, but before I can say anything Katie blurts, "But my mom's expecting you. What'll I tell her?"

"Say I got sick."

"You want me to lie?"

"Not lie exactly, just help me out."

"I can't lie to my mother."

This calls for the heavy artillery. I think hard, then say, "Look, Katie, if you don't tell your mother I'm sick, I'll tell her about you-know-what."

Katie goes white. You'd think she'd killed somebody or something instead of what she really did, which was have a quickie puff on this joint I scored. (She couldn't even hold it down, the weiner.) "You promised you'd never tell!"

"Be good and I won't," I smile, and I blow them all a kiss, pirouette and sail away.

Outside, I can't believe what I've done. I've actually blackmailed my best friend. But worse—I almost don't feel guilty!

Eight

Two days till Saturday. This is worse than waiting for Christmas. Why does time go by so slowly?

Ms. Graham is not looking too good today. Ernie Boulder has been organizing book drops, and it's getting to her. It all started when Ms. Graham made Ernie sit front-row center where she could "keep an eye on him" because he was always talking. Everyone can see him now, though, and every day when her back is turned he gives a signal and we all drop our books on the floor—BOOM—and watch her jump. She could be in the Olympics. I mean, she jumps so high I'm surprised her head doesn't go through the ceiling. I can just picture it: Ms. Graham trapped up there with her head stuck through the acoustic tiles, kicking her legs while Ernie looks up her dress.

I don't do the book drop thing. Maybe I'm turning into a suck. It's just that even if Ms. Graham is boring, she's basically okay. At least she's not mean like some other teachers, and if we're not careful she'll get sick again and who knows who we'll get for a supply.

It is *still* two days till Saturday.

Ms. Graham has written some instructions on the board. She is sitting at her desk pretending to mark, but her pen isn't moving, and neither are her eyes. She's just staring. I don't think she's going to teach today.

The other girls are *so* impressed about me being picked by Jason. Except, of course, for Ashley A-hole, who goes around pretending she'd never go out with a senior, that only a slut would do that. Eat your heart out is all I can say.

Actually, how could anyone *not* go out with Jason? The guy is terminally cool. Today when I see him in the hall he winks, points his finger at me like it's a gun, grins and mouths the word "Saturday." So I wink, point my finger at him, grin and mouth "Saturday" right back. Then we both walk away like we're spies who've just passed a message in some secret code. Did I say *walk?* I feel more like I'm floating.

Our names sound good together, too. Leslie Phillips and Jason McCready. Leslie McCready. I like McCready way more than my own last name. My family was named after a screwdriver.

This is so girlie, writing my name like I'm married to him. Talk about embarrassing. I used to see other girls do it and I'd laugh. Is true love acting stupid and not being able to stop?

I don't know. I mean, I've never been romantic like this before—not even when I was little and playing with dolls. Back in grade four, Katie's favorite thing each Saturday was marrying Barbie and Ken and having them go on honeymoons to smoochie places like Niagara Falls or the Bahamas. Except she'd never let them have sex because she said they hadn't been married long enough. Well, no smoochie getaways for me. When it was my turn to pick a honeymoon, I'd have Barbie and Ken go on adventures. They'd scuba in the bathtub. Or skydive off the balcony with serviettes taped to their hands for parachutes.

The last time we played honeymoon, Mrs. Kincaid was out getting her hair done, and I had Barbie and Ken go on an African safari in the oven. Katie screamed when they started to melt. "You murdered them!" she cried, holding the dolls in her mother's oven mitts.

It was kind of true. Barbie's eyes were running down her face, and her hair was this goo mixed in with what used to be Ken's feet. But I wasn't about to let that spoil a good honeymoon. "If they're dead, we better give them a funeral," I said. "You can be the minister and say a prayer." The idea of being a minister cheered Katie right up. She gave a long speech about Barbie's good deeds as a missionary and her tragic love for Ken and then we buried them in the garden. The next week, we dug them up and played Zombie Barbie, but that's another story.

Anyway, with Jason, I finally get what all the fuss is about. When he kissed me on the football field—well, just thinking about it gives me a funny feeling, and things start to tingle in a way that's really amazing. Believe it or not, that was my very first French kiss. The truth is, even though I'm almost sixteen, the only thing I'm experienced at is making stuff up.

Guys don't really like me for some reason. I scare them, I guess. They like to feel they're in control, but with me, let's face it, they never know what's going to come out of my mouth. (News flash: neither do I.)

This scoop would give my mom a heart attack. Every time I come home late or get caught sneaking out after she's gone to bed, she's certain it's to see some boy. I get back and there she is, sitting at the kitchen table in her housecoat. Sometimes she's Volcano Mom ("WHAT HAVE YOU BEEN UP TO, YOUNG LADY?"), but mostly she's Long-Suffering Mom, wiping away tears with a box of Kleenex, trying to make me feel guilty.

Mom is afraid I'm going to end up pregnant. She's especially worried when I come home smelling of beer. "What's his name?" she yells, as if you need a boy to get drunk. All you need is to crash a house party. "Do you know about AIDS? Do you know about condoms?" She throws such big production numbers I swear she oughta be in show business. And she's always leaving magazines around open to stories about the tragedy of teen moms. I think she watches too much Oprah.

I want to say, "Look, Mom, stop being so embarrassing." But if she gets off on worrying, let her. Besides, actually talking to her would be awful. She doesn't really want to know about my sex life any more than I want to know about hers.

With other girls, it's trickier. I can't let them think I don't have a boyfriend. So when everybody's talking about their big heartthrob, I invent one. They have names like Jerry and Trevor and Andy and are always mysterious, guys from far away who can be ditched whenever there start to be too many questions, like when's he going to drop by the school for a visit. When asked how far I've gone, I just say, "Wouldn't you like to know?" or "Guess" and let people think I'm this big make-out expert.

Katie's crowd used to come to me for advice, because they've never gone further than sweaty hand-holding and lip kissing. "Frenching!" Katie made a face. "That's so gross, I want to brush my teeth just thinking about it."

But Katie blabbed the truth about me and boys to Ashley last summer, at their stupid youth leadership training camp, and as soon as they got back Ashley ran around and told everybody else. Needless to say, the next time the topic of boys came up and I mentioned I'd met this guy called Ricky at my dad's apartment building, the girls all gave me these funny looks.

Katie turned red and her eyes popped, and right away I knew what had happened. But I didn't crack. Instead, I laughed and said in a really loud voice, "Let me guess—Ashley's pretending to be an expert on my sex life, right?" And then I turned to Ashley and practically shouted. "You are such a pathetic baby, Ashley Walker. Who are you to talk about anybody? You can't even say the word 'penis.' Say it, Ashley! *Penis, penis, penis!!!*"

Seeing as we were hanging around the mall at the time, I got a lot of attention. I also made Ashley cry. In fact, I made her cry for a couple of weeks after that, because the next day I snuck into the guy's washroom at Mister Pizza's and wrote on the wall in Magic Marker, "For a good time call Ashley Walker" and her phone number. Serves her right.

Getting even was one thing, but I still felt really worried about what the other girls thought. That's why Frenching with Jason in broad daylight was extra fantastic.

Jason, you are my dream come true. But now I have something new to worry about: will I be *his* dream come true?

He'll probably be expecting me to be experienced, and I'm still wondering how far is too far on a first date? In one of Ann Landers's columns, which Mom *so* considerately put in front of my orange juice one morning, it said, "Guys don't buy books they can take out of the library." But even bookstores let guys take books off the shelf. The real question is, how many chapters do you let them read?

Worrying about what to do is bad enough. But even

worse is worrying about *how* to do it. Even simple stuff like kissing. That time on the football field doesn't count, because it happened so fast and out of the blue I didn't have a chance to tense up. But knowing it's coming is a different story.

Your reputation can get ruined in one night. Back in grade eight, Rachel Moses didn't do anything the first time she got kissed, just opened her mouth. Ever since, guys have called her "Slug Tongue." And then there's Debby Grace. She bit into Tommy Singh's lip so bad it bled and swelled up. So now she's "Cannibal Girl." How a person kisses can affect their whole life.

Maybe I should stay home from school tomorrow. That way I can practice kissing in front of the bathroom mirror. Also, I can make sure I don't catch a cold. I mean Saturday has to be perfect, and kissing with a runny nose—well, can you imagine?

Nine

A runny nose. If only that had been my problem. As it is, I'm going crazy.

Jason, I have to see you. To talk to you. Does anyone else know what happened on our date?

Every time I hear people laugh, I think it's about me. And when I cross the cafeteria, I'm sure everyone's staring.

Did Jason tell? I need to know, but for three days he hasn't been at school. There's no answer at his home, either, and I must have left a zillion messages on his answering machine.

Monday morning the girls were all curious, crowding around me at my locker. "So, how was your date with Mister Stud Muffin?"

"Okay," I said.

"Just okay?" All those grinning faces. Had they heard something?

"It was great. What more do you wanna know? We saw a movie, went to a rave in some warehouse, no big deal. Geez, are you my mother?"

"What's with you?"

"Nothing."

"Katie's party was great," Ashley piped up from nowhere. "It's so much better when troublemakers stay away."

Everyone sucked in their breath, expecting me to punch her or something, which I might have done, only the five-minute bell rang and she had an excuse to run. Everyone else took off too.

Except for me.

I went to my cubicle in the second-floor washroom and thought about my date with Jason, which is all I've been doing since it happened. My mind is like this horror movie that gets to the end and then goes on automatic replay. And I can't make it stop or go away.

Sleep? Forget it. Last night I finally snuck one of Mom's pills. But even that didn't help. I'd close my eyes and the movie would start on the inside of my eyelids. Like, I'm not just having a nightmare. I'm *living* one.

There's no one I can tell without getting into trouble or having it blabbed all over. So that's why I'm writing it down. To get it out. Thank God, Ms. Graham's off for a mental break. Our supply teacher is this old bald guy. He's letting us write all class, as long as we sit quietly.

Anyway, I got to the mall early on Saturday to buy some stuff. I needed to bury the crap Mom made me pack in my knapsack because I was supposedly spending the night at Katie's: a change of clothes, toiletries, a towel.

I do the mall tour, cramming my knapsack with stuff plastered with fancy brand names even a guy will recognize. I figure I can always return them the next day, or guilt Dad into an advance next time I see him. Once he hears I have a boyfriend, I figure he'll use that as an excuse to ditch our Sundays for more time with Brenda. Fine, providing he buys off his conscience with a little cash.

Last but not least, I buy a fancy shopping bag for my new rave gear: this wild, frilly, fluorescent pink-and-lime baby-doll number, plus a white Day-Glo boa and a cheap blonde beehive wig. When I add my sparkle makeup and orange eyelashes, I hope I'll have Jason creaming his jeans.

Then I look at my watch. It's 5:30. I stake out Taco Bell from a table behind a pillar at the opposite end of the food court. That way I'll be able to see Jason when he arrives without him thinking I've gotten there early. I can also check myself out in my trusty compact mirror.

I end up peeking at the mirror every two minutes, making little makeup corrections, then wondering if the corrections are too much or too little, then smudging things, fixing smudges. It's unbelievable.

Pretty soon it's 6:00 and then 6:05 and then 6:10, and then ohmigod it's 6:15! Panic attack! What if he came and I was staring at my compact and he didn't see me and he left?

I start to sweat. I tell myself to stop; all sweating will do is wreck my makeup. That thought gets me even more flustered and I start to sweat all over. Fanning my armpits just makes things worse. And now it's 6:25.

That's it—he's come and gone. He thinks I stood him up. Or what if he stood *me* up? Or he's waiting at a different Taco Bell? I'm soaking now, except for my throat, which is dry.

I take a sip of Coke. Suddenly somebody taps my shoulder from behind. I jump. Coke goes out my nose. I whirl around and it's him. I'm wiping my face with serviettes and my makeup's ruined and he's laughing.

"It's not funny!"

"Sorry." But he's still laughing.

"I thought we'd missed each other."

He points to the Tower store behind me. "I've been back there the whole time."

"Why didn't you come over?"

"I was enjoying myself."

"Doing what?"

"Watching."

He's smiling, so I smile too, only I don't really get the joke. Then I say, "So, do you want to grab some burritos or something? What time's the movie?"

"There isn't going to be a movie," he says. "I've got a surprise."

The surprise is his folks are up at their cottage. His dad is this fancy lawyer in something called Mergers and Acquisitions, and he just finished putting together a major real estate deal. His parents decided to take off at the last minute, which means Jason has the house to himself. The idea of being alone with him gets me a little nervous. But also a little excited.

Next thing I know, he's got my stuff stashed on his motorcycle and I'm sitting behind him holding on like crazy. I've never been on a motorcycle before, and the wind in my face is scary and wonderful all at the same time. Plus the feel of my hands on his stomach is making my insides melt. I keep saying to myself, "Concentrate, Leslie. Concentrate or you could die"—not because I think we're going to crash or anything, but because I'm afraid I'm going to faint off his bike into traffic.

His house is in a really nice neighborhood, the kind with trees and a park, where everybody cuts their grass. There's a Camry in the driveway. I wonder if his folks have stayed home after all but he says no, that's his mom's. His parents always travel in his dad's BMW.

He parks beside the attached garage and helps me off the motorcycle. I have my knapsack on my back, but he carries my bag with the rave costume. I mean, he's actually carrying my stuff. Nobody's ever done that before, except for Katie the time I busted my collarbone.

When we get inside, I ask, "How come you go to our school when you live here?"

The answer's original, just like him. He went to a private school in Port Burdock, real snobby, and he was on all the teams. Everybody was after him because he was this big sports star, though, and it all got to be too much. He tried quitting the teams, but they wouldn't let him because he was on an athletic scholarship. So he said, "Fine. I'm dropping out." And he did, just like that, and came to our school where nobody'd know him. I'd give anything to be popular. But Jason's the exact opposite: he just wants to be himself.

By the time he's finished giving me a tour of the upstairs, it's pretty clear his folks are loaded. The master bedroom has a fireplace and a wall-screen TV, not to mention a private bathroom with a sunken Jacuzzi.

For a second, I wonder if there's a reason we've ended up in the bedroom. Is he planning to make a move? I'm half scared and half hoping, but he's a perfect gentleman. "That's it," he says, and ushers me downstairs. I'm sort of disappointed, but also glad I can relax.

"Can I get you something to drink?" he asks as we hit the kitchen.

"Sure. Do you have a Coke?"

He gives me a look. "Let me rephrase that," and his lip twitches. "Can I get you something to *drink?*"

My heart skips. I've never had a drink alone with a guy before, and even if he can behave himself, I'm not sure I can. All the same, I don't want to look stupid and I figure *one* can't do any harm, so I say, "What do you have?"

He grins. Then, instead of just saying beer, wine, rum or whatever, he starts reciting labels: "Johnnie Walker, Smirnoff, Gilbey's, Havana Club: your wish is my command."

Seeing as I'm not sure what half those brands are, I decide to play it safe. I say, "I'll have what you're having."

"Johnnie Walker on the rocks," he says, and he takes a couple of tumblers out of the cupboard, shoots in a few cubes from the ice machine on the fridge and pours. Johnnie Walker I've at least heard of. I know it's scotch. The kind they serve in the movies.

Jason hands me the drink and phones out for pizza while I have a sip. I almost choke. It's not like beer at all. I mean, it's puke foul. Who invented this stuff? All the same, if I don't finish it, I'll look like a reject. I know if I sip slowly I'll start retching, so I make a quick decision. I stop breathing and swallow it in two big gulps. It almost comes back up, but I just focus on Jason's butt as he slouches at the counter by the telephone, and the sick feeling goes away.

Jason hangs up. He sees my empty glass. He's impressed. "You sure know how to knock it back."

"I was thirsty," I say.

"I better freshen that up, then," he says, pouring me another. Seeing as I've just made out I love the stuff, I can't very well say no.

We spend the next half hour talking about parents and teachers and kids at school, and I discover that scotch is a lot like swimming in the lake in May: it's okay once you get used to it.

Jason pours me a third. It doesn't taste so bad any more.

By the fourth, I'm telling him about Katie's slumber party. He finds the idea of slumber parties hilarious, especially the part about facials and fashion shows. I tell him how I hate Ashley. He says I'm way out of the league of all those girls. They're just kids, and I'm practically a woman. Coming from a senior who had his pick at Port Burdock, that's saying something.

When the pizza arrives, he says, "Let's eat down in the rec room."

I stand up. I fall back in my chair. "Whoa, what did they put in that scotch?"

"Scotch," he says, which for some reason we both find majorly funny.

"I think I better stick to beer."

He gets me a beer and we go down to his rec room, which is huge, with wood paneling and parquet everywhere. It's full of stuff—leather furniture and a pool table and a dart board and another wall-screen TV and a sound system. It's even got its very own mini-bar. Not to mention a bathroom. I go in and splash my face with cold water, because I'm starting to feel a bit out of it.

I have a slight gap in my memory after that. We must have eaten the pizza, because I remember being back in the bathroom throwing up. I think the puking was after we smoked the joint, because that's when we decided we were too wasted to drive to the rave and we'd just stay in his rec room. We started doing a little kissing too. After all my worrying, kissing didn't make me feel tense at all. It made me feel great.

Then, just when I was all relaxed, Jason started to undo my pants. I said, "Maybe we should take a break." He said, "Why?" And I said, thinking fast, "So I can show you the stuff I bought at the mall." Jason got this smile on his face and joked how if I wasn't going to be doing a fashion show at Katie's, maybe I should do a fashion show for him. I said, "Really?" And he went, "Yeah. I'd like that. Watching's fun."

Jason starts blasting techno out of the sound system, and suddenly I'm back in party mode. I go into the bathroom to change, then make my big entrance. It's dark. Jason's turned the lights way down and switched on this color wheel. Reds, greens and yellows swirl around the room. It's like we have our own private rave.

Jason's on the couch, and I'm prancing up and down in front of him in my new outfit, twirling the Day-Glo boa. I feel sexy, like a professional dancer. And then for some reason I step back into the pool table and trip, and all of a sudden I'm really woozy.

The next thing I know, the music's off, the lights are bright and Jason's yelling, "Get dressed. You gotta get out of here."

I'm squinting. I'm cold. Oh my God, I'm naked! My clothes are all over the floor. There's blood. What's going on?

Jason's pulling my dress on, tossing me my boa. I try to say something, only it's like I can't speak. Jason's wiping the floor with a towel and spraying air freshener. He starts hauling me up the stairs by my armpits.

He drops me at the landing, runs back for my knapsack, shoves twenty bucks in my hand. "I've called a cab to meet you at the end of the street. Now go!" He pushes me out the door, tossing my knapsack after me. It's like a bad dream. I'm wide awake and I'm still asleep and I'm running down the street. I get to the corner. I slump on the curb. I don't know if I pass out again, only there's lights. It's a cab. I get inside.

It's two-thirty when the cab drops me off at my apartment building. I can't go upstairs; I'm supposed to be at Katie's. So I do the only thing I can think of. I go down to the laundry room.

It's bright fluorescents, old machines, scuffed walls and cracked linoleum. But at least I'll be alone in there. Which is good, because I start to notice I feel sore all over. And I have this throbbing ache. Down there.

When I reach down, there's blood and stuff caked on the inside of my legs. And that's when it hits me. That's when I realize what's happened. Or what I think happened. Because I don't know. I can't remember.

The laundry tub is at the end of the machines. I take off everything and wash myself everywhere, drying myself with my new top. Once I'm dry, I put on the clothes Mom made me pack for Katie's, which are in a plastic bag at the bottom of my knapsack. The rest of the stuff I dump in a washer.

I'm not taking those things home. I'm tying them in that plastic bag and tossing them in the garbage. But first I need them clean. I mean, what if someone finds them? What if they see the stains? It's like I've committed a crime.

And know what the worst part is? If I'd been awake and sober, I would have said yes.

Ten

After writing that down, I had to run to the washroom. My eyes were gushing, and no way I wanted anyone to see me cry. I stayed in my cubicle till I figured everyone was gone for the day.

I figured wrong. As I walk down the hall, I see Katie, Ashley and a couple of other girls hanging around, pretending to be minding their own business. But what they're really minding is the fancy envelope taped to the outside of my locker door.

I open it and take out the card. It's got a picture of a cartoon lion doing somersaults. Inside, it says, "You Drive Me Wild! No Lyin'!" Underneath is a handwritten note: "I had a great time Saturday. Hope you did too. I'm out back catching a few rays on the bleachers. J."

The card—it's so *casual.* First I think, am I crazy? Did I just imagine everything? And then I remember the blood, the pain. My face goes flushed all of a sudden, and I'm mad. I mean, what planet is this guy on?

When I look up, the girls are staring at me, and for one horrible second I think this is a repeat of a year ago, before my folks split, back in the time when I was more or less normal.

I'd made the big mistake of trying out for the junior cheerleading team. Needless to say, I didn't make it. Like—duh—to be a cheerleader you have to be cute and perky and able to do the splits without falling over. All the same, when the list went up on the phys. ed. bulletin board, I was crushed. While all the Cute and Perkies were jumping up and down squealing, me and the other losers hung around like a bad smell, congratulating everyone and pretending to smile.

When I got to school the next day, there was this typed letter from Ms. Patrick, the cheerleading coach, stuck in the crack of my locker. It said how there'd been a mistake and how my name should have been on the list and how I should show up for the first practice that night after school.

I was practically bouncing off the walls all day. I told

everybody. I even phoned home and left a message on the machine for Mom and Dad. After school I was the first one into the change room.

But no sooner had we gotten lined up outside on the track than Ms. Patrick stopped and hollered out, "Leslie Phillips, what are you doing here?"

"I came like you asked in the letter."

There were titters everywhere. Ms. Patrick said she'd like to speak to me in private and got Lara Babson, Queen of the Cute and Perkies, to lead warmup exercises while she walked me to her office. Everybody was staring. Katie, too, who'd come to cheer me from the sidelines.

Inside, I showed Ms. Patrick the letter. She said I should have known it was fake since there was no handwritten signature. Also, that if there'd been a mistake she'd have mentioned it during morning announcements and added my name to the posted list along with her initials. She made it sound like the whole thing was my fault.

Then she asked who I thought could have done it. I just stared at the floor and shrugged. Who'd done it was the last thing on my mind. All I was thinking about was how I was going to explain to all the people I'd told that I wasn't on the team after all. That I was a sucker, a loser, a reject.

When I see the girls watching me read the card, all these awful feelings come back. And I think, "It's a set-up! They want to see me run out to the bleachers so they can laugh at me!"

But then Katie says, "Is it from him?" and my fears disappear. Because Katie would never hurt me like that. Here I was about to cry, and now all I want to do is laugh, because Katie's acting as excited as a new puppy meeting house guests. I mean, I want to tell her not to wet the floor. Instead, I smile mysteriously and say, "Maybe." That gets the girls even more giddy. Except for Ashley, who looks as if she just sucked a bug.

"What's he say?" Katie pants.

"Who cares?" snaps Ashley. "Look, if we don't get a move on we'll be late for choir practice."

Katie gives me one of her patented hand flaps and starts running down the hall after Ms. A-Hole. At the corner she turns and calls back, "Phone me? Okay?"

"Whatever," I say, as if I have *much* more important things to do. Then I wink at the other girls, fan myself with my card and waltz down the corridor.

When I get to the door leading out to the track, I can see him lounging on top of the bleachers. School's been out for a while now, but he's waited. It's like he knew I would come.

There's no football practice today. Jason and I are alone except for one or two track-types doing laps. I walk across the field. I climb halfway up the bleachers and stop. He must have heard me clunking on the boards but he keeps his eyes closed like he did the day we first met. Laid out in the sun, he looks sweet and innocent.

All of a sudden I'm scared. Not of *him,* exactly. It's just that, well, since Saturday I've been crazy to talk to him, but now that he's here I don't know what to say. What I say is, "So . . ."

He opens his eyes, turns his head towards me and flashes this slow easy smile. "What a perfect day."

I nod and force myself not to look away. "I got your card."

"So I see." There's a pause. He sits up, still smiling.

"Where've you been?"

"Out of town with my folks. They took me back to the cottage. I meant to call. Sorry."

"That's okay." I stare at my feet.

"So what are you doing down there, stranger?" He pats the bench beside him. "Come on up here."

I stay where I am. I take a deep breath, then say, "If you wanted to talk to me, how come you didn't meet me at my locker?"

He looks surprised. "Isn't it nicer having a bit of privacy? I mean, those friends of yours . . ." He shakes his head as if we've escaped from a bunch of baby sisters.

"Maybe it's nicer," I hesitate. And then I blurt out, "Or maybe you were scared I'd start yelling in front of them."

"Yelling?" He laughs. "What about?"

"You know." I hear my voice start to tremble so I shut up. I stare at his nose like I do with Mr. Carrouthers. Only he doesn't have any nose hairs that I can see. He looks perfect, and I feel confused.

Jason doesn't blink. His eyebrows scrunch up like he's

concentrating, puzzled, and I wonder—can he really not remember? Or have I made a mistake? Did nothing happen after all?

"Jason..." I say at last in a voice so small I'm hardly breathing, "...did we?"

For a split second time stops, and for some bizarre reason I have a flash of driving with Dad when this bird swooped in front of the car and everything went into slow motion and I was praying my head off the bird would escape and then THUMP. I hear Jason say, "Yeah." But the way he says it, it sounds like "So what?"

And now I'm just standing there like a dummy with tears sliding off my face.

"Hey," Jason says. His voice is all concerned, as if he's trying to comfort me, only what he's saying is, "Why the tears? It's not like you were a virgin or anything." He starts coming down as if he wants to comfort me, only I bet it's just so the track guys don't start staring.

"Stay away." I wave my hands.

"But I don't get it," he says. "I mean, it was your idea."

My idea? Am I really hearing this?

"I thought we should wait," he says. "You know, make it special. But you kept going, 'Now is special. Now.' Don't you remember?"

The truth is, I don't. But surely I would have remembered that.

"Leslie, you've gotta believe me." His voice is so sincere. "I'd never do anything to hurt you."

"Oh no? Well, what about the money? You made me feel like a ho."

"My folks got called back to town because Dad's deal was falling apart. It was after midnight. They phoned ahead to let me know they were coming, so I wouldn't think they were burglars or something."

I'm sniffling, but I'm listening.

"Leslie, please, you *gotta* remember. We wanted you to make a good first impression. But you were so wasted—we both were—we thought you should leave, come back to meet them another time. I paid for the cab, sure, but what was I supposed to do? I felt responsible. And I was way too drunk to drive."

I look in his eyes, and there is so much pain there it breaks my heart. Suddenly I feel ashamed. How could I have thought those terrible things about him? I was zoned out of my mind, and he took care of me. I should be thanking him instead.

"Leslie, I have feelings for you. I mean it. If I've done or said anything to upset you, I'm sorry." He's all helpless now, like he's begging me to forgive him. How could I be so wrong?

"Did you mean it about meeting your folks?"

"Yeah. Unless you don't want to."

"No. That'd be fantastic."

He kisses me gently on the eyelids and whispers, "Let's go, then."

I wash my face before heading out. I also change into

the Mom-Approved-Clothes stashed in my locker, in case Mrs. McCready has a thing against vinyl mini-skirts. When I'm done, I don't exactly look like a nun, but I look decent enough not to scare anybody.

As it turns out, though, I'm not the one who needs to worry about looking decent. When we get to Jason's house, it's like Saturday: the Camry's in the drive but the BMW is missing. Jason says his dad must still be at work. Inside, the place is quiet as a tomb. For a second I wonder if coming over was such a good idea. Then, from upstairs, I hear this voice. It sounds like a movie star, all husky and glamorous. "Is that you, Doug?"

"No, it's me, Mom."

"I am so annoyed with your father," the Voice exhales. It sounds like it's coming down the stairs. "He promised he'd be home early. We're supposed to be at the Richardsons' in an hour and he hasn't even phoned."

Now I see the Voice, and it sees me. I'm not sure who is more surprised.

Mrs. McCready could be a model. She's tall with a long neck, designer hair and an amazing figure. But there's something wrong with the picture. She's in her slip, with a mud mask on her face and a glass of tomato juice in her hand.

"This is Leslie. Leslie, this is my mom."

Mrs. McCready decides to pretend everything's normal. "How do you do?" she nods, then tilts her chin at Jason. "You didn't mention we'd be having company. Your father and I are going out."

"We're working on a geography project for school tomorrow. We'll be down in the rec room."

She considers this briefly. "Good. There's pie in the fridge if you get hungry."

Before I know it, Jason and I are heading downstairs.

"Does your mom really think we're in the same grade?" I whisper.

"My mom doesn't think at all after three o'clock." He winks. I don't get it. "Leslie, wake up. You think that's just tomato juice she's drinking?"

"But she acts so sober."

"Practice makes perfect." He puts his arms around me and grins. "Speaking of practice . . . "

I start to resist, but the kiss is so nice I start kissing him back. My eyes are closed, and I see little flashes of light. It feels like that first day on the football field, only better.

After a few minutes, Jason breaks away. He goes into the bathroom and brings back a towel, folding it carefully in the middle of the sofa.

"What's that for?"

"You're my girlfriend, aren't you?"

His girlfriend? Wow! "Yeah, I guess so."

"Well . . . " He flashes that smile and sweeps his arm towards the sofa as if he's a waiter directing me to my seat in some fancy restaurant. "It's not like we haven't before."

It's sort of true. I mean, the damage has already been done, and if we're officially going out, well . . . All the same, I feel weird. "Your mother is upstairs."

"So we'll keep quiet. Besides, she only hears what she wants to hear. Hey, if it'll make you feel any better..." He turns and puts on a CD.

"But what if she comes down?"

"She won't. She doesn't like surprises." I'm still not sure about things, but I melt when he looks deep in my eyes and whispers, "I love you, you know."

Somehow we're on the sofa, and then, well, things go so fast I hardly know it's happened, except I hurt. We're even still dressed, except for my panties are around my knees and my sweater's pulled up. All of a sudden I want to get out of there. How can I be so in love and still feel like shit?

"I should go," I say. "My mom'll be expecting me."

"Sure." He nods, as if he's secretly happy. "I'll drive you back."

In the living room, Mrs. McCready is dressed in something out of *Vogue,* still holding her tomato juice. She stares through the picture window. "Finished your project?"

"Yeah."

"You must be a good influence on him," she says to me. Her eyelid twitches.

It's six-thirty by the time I get home. There's salad and a plate of cold macaroni and cheese waiting for me on the kitchen table. My mom is waiting too.

"Where were you?" she asks.

"Over at Katie's."

"Is that so."

From the tone of her voice, I'm not sticking around to chat. I head down the hall to my room, calling back, "Yeah. We were working on a project for school tomorrow. You have a problem with that?"

Mom follows me. "Yes, I have a problem with that," she fires back. "If you were at Katie's, perhaps you'd like to explain why she called from choir practice asking you to phone her about some card."

"None of your business."

"As long as you live with me, everything is my business."

"Go to hell!" I yell. And I slam the door in her face.

Eleven

One of Mom's favorite expressions is "Let sleeping dogs lie." She says this all the time when I ask her about Dad and other women: "Leslie, just let sleeping dogs lie."

I joke, "Does that mean I should let Dad lie, on account of he's a sleeping dog?"

She gives me a dirty look. "I mean, don't bring up unpleasant topics from the past. Okay?"

Fine, so Mom doesn't have a sense of humor. But at least you'd think she'd practice what she preaches. Isn't it her job to set an example? I figured a good night's sleep and she'd drop the whole Sherlock Holmes routine about where I was last night. But no. Seven o'clock her alarm goes off, and she's still on the case.

Well, if she's going to be a busybody, I'm going to be a bitch.

"For the last time, Leslie, where were you?"

"Wherever will make you happy."

Pretty soon it's eight, and she's so wired from her coffee and my crap she's running in circles like a hamster on speed. I'm sitting over bran flakes while she screams at me from the bathroom—brushing her teeth with one hand, spraying deodorant with the other—when somebody buzzes from the lobby.

"Will you see who it is?"

"I'm eating my breakfast."

"Leslie, I'm late enough for work as it is."

Whoever's in the lobby buzzes again. Mom runs out of the bathroom, toothpaste drooling off her chin. "Yes?" she hollers into the intercom. She mouths at me: "You're grounded."

"Annabelle Florists," says this voice.

Mom looks surprised. So do I. "Come on up."

The delivery guy arrives in no time. He hands her a bundle done up in fancy wrapping paper. Inside, there are a dozen long-stemmed red roses and a note. Mom reads: "Leslie. Thanks for a great geography lesson. J."

She passes the roses to me. I'm in another world. I cradle the bouquet like it's a baby.

Mom is not impressed. "So I take it *he's* where you were last night."

"Somebody's just sent me roses for the first time in my life. Can't you be happy?"

"Does 'somebody' have a name?" She wipes the tooth-paste off her mouth.

"Why do you always have to spoil everything?" Instead of fighting, I want to cry. I sit back down in my chair and bury my head so she won't see.

"Pooky Bear..."

"Don't call me that."

"I'm sorry."

I feel her hand on my shoulder and shake it off.

"Look, I'm happy for you. I just don't like you sneaking around behind my back."

I wait until I'm sure my voice won't break. "His name is Jason McCready."

"Have you been seeing him for a long time?"

"Who says I've been seeing him?"

Mom takes a deep breath, smoothes her clothes and sets a stool under the cupboard over the stove. "How be I get the vase and we put those flowers in some water?"

"You're going to be late for work."

"This is more important."

Out comes my great-grandmother's crystal vase and we're cutting the ends of the stems with a kitchen knife, arranging the roses, starting to have a good time, even. It's your basic Kodak Moment. Half of me feels wonderful, and the other half wants to gag.

"They're beautiful." Mom smiles.

"Yeah." I want to shut up now, but suddenly I have this overwhelming need to say his name. "Jason's great. The other girls are really jealous." Saying his name out loud felt good. So good, I forget Mom only acts nice when she wants something. She doesn't let me forget for long.

"Why don't you invite Jason over?"

Thunk. "*Here?*"

"What's the matter with here?"

"Mother, please. Are you trying to humiliate me?"

"I beg your pardon?"

I roll my eyes. And—bang—it's like the last five minutes never existed.

"Don't tell me you're ashamed of your own home."

"Aren't you?"

Mom kind of slumps. She puts the stool away, folds the fancy wrapping paper, and drops the stem ends in the garbage. I feel horrible.

"It's nothing personal, Mom," I say. "It's just, well, Jason's parents are important, like his dad does big business deals and everything, and they live in this enormous house and everything is new and expensive."

I get treated to her Mom-on-a-Cross face. "You know, Leslie, it takes more than money to make a home."

Pass me the barf bag. "I never said a home is only money," I shoot back. "A home's also supposed to be a place where people love each other. But I don't see a lot of that around here either."

I want Mom to say something. I want her to yell at me, even. But she doesn't. She just puts her coat on slowly and heads out to work.

Twelve

When I get to school, Jason is there at my locker waiting for me. Leaning against the lockers across from mine, actually, in his leather jacket and shades. It's like he's sunning himself indoors.

"Hi," I say, loud enough for everyone to hear. "Thanks for the roses."

He gives me a kiss. Just sort of drapes over me with his hands on my bum. I feel self-conscious but also proud, because this way people will know we're together.

"I came to walk you to class. Get your stuff. We'll be late."

Everybody's looking at us, and my head bobs like one of Aunt Betty's knick-knack china Dutch girls. I can't help myself. I scramble my books out of my locker with a wink at Katie. Then, without looking where I'm going, I bump right into him.

"Hey, if it isn't the Leslie doll," he laughs. "Wind her up, she walks into a wall." I hear a few titters and just about die, but not for long. In one smooth move, he slides his arm across my shoulder. I put my free hand into his back pocket—up yours, Ashley—and together we float off to class.

We're together at lunch, too, just us on the bleachers. I tell him about the grilling I got from Mom and how he's lucky to have a mother who minds her own business. He

LESLIE'S JOURNAL • **65**

smiles and says something that blows me away: he thinks this meeting-my-mom bit is a good idea.

"Why not?" he winks. "It'll help keep her onside."

I guess "onside" is the kind of word you pick up around the dinner table when your dad is important. But how did he get so smart at psychology?

Then he asks if I'd like to see Pigjam next Friday.

"Aren't they sold out?"

"No sweat, I got contacts," he says. "The show's at eight, I'll pick you up around seven. That way I can meet your mom and we'll have an excuse to split quick."

He's brilliant.

Who is not brilliant is Katie. She and the group are on their way back from Mister Pizza's, and she's seen us. The rest of the girls go into the school, but Katie heads towards us with a goofy grin on her face.

I start sending her these very strong Stay-Away-Katie vibes. But apparently the only messages Katie picks up come from God or something, because she sure doesn't get mine. She comes right up to Jason and me and smiles, like I'm supposed to welcome her into our private conversation. I don't.

"Yeah?"

"I just thought I'd come over and say hi." She grins and gives this little girlie finger wave. "You must be Jason."

"And who must you be?" he says, polite and sarcastic all at once.

"Katie. I've heard so much about you."

"And I've heard so much about you."

"Oh yeah?" Katie's face lights up like she's in kindergarten and the teacher's put a big gold star on her forehead.

Wake up, Katie, I think. He's insulting you. Don't you get it? Why don't you leave us alone? But it's too late. Jason's getting ready to leave.

"I'd love to stay and chat," he says, "but I've got things to do." I go to follow him, but he holds up his hand. "You stay with your pal Katie here. I'll catch you later." He walks off without looking back.

Katie is all moon-eyed. You'd think she just talked to a movie star or something. But me, I'm heartsick. Jason and I were having such a good time, and she had to go and scare him away. A wave of anger surges up inside me, and I decide to let her have it. But right when I'm ready to let rip, Katie blurts out, "So, are you guys doing it?"

My heart skips. "Who says we're doing it?"

Katie looks at my face and gasps. "Oh no, you *are!*"

"I never said that!" I shout. "I asked you, 'Who says?'"

"Nobody."

"*Nobody?*"

"Okay. Ashley. She says that's why Jason's started to hang around."

"What a bitch."

"Well, *are* you?"

"If Jason and I were doing it, do you think I'd tell *you?*"

"Yeah. Why not?"

"You can't keep your mouth shut, that's why not."

"Are you still mad I told Ashley you made up boy-friends?"

"Among other things."

"What other things?"

"Last night you told my mom you were at choir practice. I told her I was at your place. You got me in so much trouble—"

"It's not my fault you lied to your mother."

"And it's not my fault you're a moron."

Katie's eyes get full. "Leslie, why are you yelling at me? What's the matter? We used to be friends."

"Used to be!" And now I pounce. "Used-to-be's right, isn't it? And I suppose that's my fault. All I know is I used to have a friend I could count on, but now she only has time for my worst enemy. Well, I don't care. I have a boy-friend who loves me and I don't need to waste my time with a nerdy moron who needs her mother's permission to go to the bathroom."

Katie's face disintegrates. I watch as she turns and runs across the grass, shoulders heaving.

Serves her right. I've never let anyone come between us—not parents, not friends, nobody. So how come she's the one acting hurt? All the same, I feel like a turd.

By the time I get to math class, I'm not mad any more. I pull out a sheet of plain paper, write a note and slip it on Katie's desk while Mr. Kogawa is at the board. It says, "You'll always be my best friend, no matter what." There's a little pause, and then Katie turns around with a look so serious I don't know whether to laugh or cry. Then she whispers, "Me too," and I know which: I cry.

Thirteen

*E*ven after I made up with Katie, I was still worried that she might have wrecked things between me and Jason. I had this bizarro panic when he walked away from the bleachers that he *wasn't* going to catch me later, that he'd actually left for good.

One of the horrible things about dating guys is, all of a sudden, out of the blue, for no reason, they just stop calling you. It's BANG: one minute you're their girlfriend and the next minute you aren't. And they won't even say why. It's like they're afraid to face you and have you get mad at them. So there's always this scary feeling in the back of your mind. At the same time they're smiling and laughing with you, they may be planning to split. I know I'm talking like a sudden expert and all. But you don't have to watch a talk show to prove what I'm saying—just ask any girl in my school.

But Jason is different. Not only did he catch me later, he was at my locker right after class.

We went and studied at his place. (Well, okay, we didn't really study.) Since then, Jason has wanted to see me every single night. He even said he's afraid to let me out of his sight. Is that romantic or what? He's meeting me after school today and tomorrow too, and then it's Friday and the Pigjam concert.

As for Mom, Jason's little psychology trick worked great. I told her he wanted to meet her this weekend, and she chilled right out. She said if I wanted to study at his place she'd hold supper for me—"I'm glad you're finally starting to do some homework!"—as long as I was back by seven and his mom was home.

"Deal," I said. "Oh, and before he comes, will you help me tidy the place up?"

As soon as I said that she got this amused grown-up look.

"What's so funny?"

"If *you* want to tidy up, he must be *very* special."

I hate it when Mom does that. It's like I'm a baby or something, this cute little pet put on the earth to entertain her. It was especially annoying this time, because she was getting even for all the times I've been a slob. Last year she was always complaining about how my room was a pigsty. I told her if it bothered her so much she should stop looking at it. That's when I got the "Keep Out" sign.

But who cares? Mom can have her little joke if it keeps her from asking questions. Let's face it, if she knew the truth about me and Jason, she'd have a heart attack. Maybe even kick off.

Just thinking about Mom being dead gives me a nervous breakdown. Dad might as well be worm meat; he's pretty much out of my life these days. If Mom was gone too, I don't know what I'd do. Sometimes I imagine myself literally screaming my lungs inside out or throwing myself out a window or stabbing myself to death with the hedge clippers. (Actually, those got sold in the yard sale before we moved into the apartment.)

Worrying that Mom might die because of something I did drives me crazy. That's what I'm worrying about when I step into English today. And—speaking of nervous breakdowns and going crazy—guess who's back? Ms. Graham. She's smiling like a maniac. If she doesn't watch out, her cheeks are going to explode.

The class is so dumbfounded we don't even talk, much less get rowdy. I mean, our jaws are all on the floor, and we just sort of drop into our seats and stare at her, as if she's a mirage or something.

"It's great to be back," she says. "I've missed you and I'm feeling much better, thanks, and I just know the rest of the year is going to be really special."

They better adjust her medication. Still, the tremor in her hands is mostly gone, and she's hardly sweating at all. That is, until she asks how many of us filled out our *To Kill a Mockingbird* question and answer sheets. We look at her all innocent, like we haven't a clue what she's talking about.

"You mean while I've been gone you haven't done *anything?* Why, every day you were to read twenty pages and answer a sheet of questions. I left instructions!"

Was she born simple, or does she work at it? The average supply teacher has a hard time figuring out how to turn on a TV. You think they can follow instructions? And when it's a regular teacher supervising, why should *they* care? They have a million students of their own to worry about.

Ms. Graham starts rummaging around in her filing cabinet, still smiling but definitely getting twitchy. "The handouts were right here. Oh dear." And now it looks like she's having a near-death experience because guess what? The Handouts Are Missing! Her eyes do that gerbil thing, and you can see her trying to figure out what's happened. Did she actually forget to make them? Is her memory of them a hallucination? Or maybe one of the janitors broke in and stole them?

Naturally, the handouts aren't missing at all: the truth is, aside from a couple of goofs, most of the supply teachers really *did* give them to us. The sheets just didn't get done. But we never did them when she was here, so why would we start while she was away? Ms. Graham is too goodhearted. She gives our class credit for giving a shit. Can she really have forgotten what we're like? Has she got Alzheimer's or something?

When she was away, the guys at the back played cards as always, and the rest of us either caught up on our other homework or stared out the window or wrote in our journals. I also read the book, but only because I wanted to. (It would be nice to have a dad like Atticus instead of the loser I got stuck with. I mean, I can't even *imagine* Atticus trading his daughter for a slut like Brenda.)

Anyway, things are starting to get really interesting when

Cindy Williams puts up her hand. "Are these the handouts, Ms. Graham?" she asks, all dimples and curls. She holds up a binder full of neatly completed question and answer sheets. (Cindy gets straight As, and she writes with big fat letters and signs her name with a little heart over the "i." She makes me gag.)

"So you *did* receive the handouts!" Ms. Graham exclaims, and she's back on her spaceship to Planet Happy. "Good, good." She hops to her desk. "That means you're all prepared for a little content quiz."

Before you can say "Boo Radley," Ms. Graham's handed out this test full of multiple choices and fill-in-the-blanks. It takes about two minutes, and then she collects them and gives us our journals. We're supposed to write while she marks.

We don't write very long before Ms. Graham calls us to attention. It seems only about four or five people have bothered to read the book. Most of the content quizzes are either blank or have supposedly funny remarks written in where the answers should go. Such as: "Jem reads <u>porno</u> to <u>dead gophers</u>."

That one's courtesy of Ernie Boulder. Ms. Graham reads it out loud to make him look stupid. But instead, the card players at the back hoot "Aw right!" and Ernie bows as if he's a hero or something.

Ms. Graham is losing it. "There are only two of you mature enough to call yourselves grade ten students," she yells. "Cindy Williams and Leslie Phillips. Because they did their work, they each received a perfect score. I trust the rest of you will learn from their example."

Waydego, Ms. Graham. I mean, can I die now?

Then the biggest unfairness of all. She announces she's going to give everyone a second chance, and she tosses the tests in the recycling bin. Unbelievable. She goes and humiliates me, and the test isn't even going to count!

To make sure everyone is prepared for the makeup test, she says we're going to read the book aloud, up and down the aisles, half a page each from start to finish. The only good thing is, because Cindy and I read the book, we get to write in our journals instead. So for the next ten years while everyone is mumbling their way through *To Kill a Mockingbird,* I get to think about after-school "studying" and count the days to Friday, which is what I'm doing now.

Fourteen

Friday arrived like magic. Jason buzzed up right at seven. I let him in and boy, was he a knockout, gelled and manicured in a tan wool turtleneck, pressed slacks and shoes to die for.

"Parents love it when the guy's well dressed and punctual," he'd told me. Well, not Mom. When things are perfect, she gets suspicious.

I make the introductions.

"Pleased to meet you, Jason," Mom nods. She acts very polite, the sort of polite that's almost rude.

Jason ignores the attitude. "Pleasure's mine, Mrs. Phillips," he says, shaking her hand. He sounds way mature, like he sells imported cars or something.

"Leslie tells me you're going to the Pigjam concert at the Skydome. What kind of a band is Pigjam?" Translation: "There better not be drugs."

But Jason's a mind reader. "Pretty mainstream," he replies. "I don't go for heavy metal or techno."

"Good. Well, that sounds like fun, then."

"I hope so. The tickets are a fortune. Luckily, Dad managed to get us comps through a client of his."

Is Mom impressed? No way. She smiles pleasantly and says, "That's nice," like it's no big deal. What's up her nose now?

Jason looks at me, still smiling. "Is that all you're wearing? You'll catch cold."

"Okay." I'm not dressed like a slut or anything, but I've only put on enough to pass inspection. I wonder what he's up to, and then it clicks; he's out to impress Mom. I laugh and come back in my Tommy jeans and a fancy-knit sweater over top. "We gotta go, Mom, or we'll be late."

Jason opens the door for me. "There's no need to wait up, Mrs. Phillips. Your daughter's in good hands."

"Actually, Jason," Mom smiles tightly, "Leslie's well-being is in *my* hands."

"Absolutely," Jason agrees without missing a beat. Can he keep his cool or what. He shakes her hand again, and we're out the door.

Jason's got his mom's Camry. We get to the Skydome underground garage and back into a parking space against the far wall between two empty cars. I get out and start for the elevator, but Jason's fiddling with something.

"Hurry up, we're going to be late."

"Relax. The opening act'll take an hour."

And now I see what he's doing. He's folded out one of those cardboard sunscreens and put it across the front windshield. He opens the door to the back seat.

"Jason! Not here!"

"No, something else, dummy," he says. "I've got something for you."

"Can't you give it to me out here?"

But I get in the back seat anyway and Jason pulls out a joint. "Grade A. No kidding. I got it off a special friend."

"What if we get busted?"

"Who's going to check third-basement parking? We're at the end, cars on either side, a screen up. Come on, you're acting like that Katie geek."

We have the joint, but instead of feeling giggly, I start getting paranoid. Especially when he puts his hand up my sweater. I knew this was going to happen.

"Jason, you said we wouldn't. I mean, we're in public!"

"It'll be exciting. Trust me."

As if.

Jason has me back home at five minutes before twelve. He doesn't come in.

As usual Mom's waiting up, only instead of sitting at the kitchen table, she's in the living room with her back to me, watching some old movie.

It's creepy. She doesn't say a word. There's just this low sound of voices coming from the TV and her sitting absolutely still.

For a minute, I think maybe she's fallen asleep. That'd be perfect. Because I don't want to get close to her before having a shower.

But just as I reach the door of the bathroom, she says in a loud voice, "How was the concert?"

"Fine," I say. I'm trying to sound cheerful, but my throat is tight. Before she has a chance to say anything else, I scoot inside and close the door.

Mom is still waiting for me when I come out wrapped in a towel. She's turned the TV off and is sitting at the table. "Leslie, could I speak to you for a minute?" She's not mad. She sounds strange, like I better say yes or there's really going to be trouble.

"Okay," I say. "Just let me put something on."

I come back in track pants and a top.

Mom sits still for a minute and then says: "Leslie, how old is Jason?"

"I don't know."

"Don't you think it would be better if you dated someone more your own age?"

"What, I'm a baby or something? Or he's this old-man-pervert child molester?"

"No."

"Then what?"

Mom looks at me very seriously. "Honey, I don't know how to put this..."

"Don't bother. I knew you wouldn't like him. I mean, if God asked me for a date you'd find something to complain about. Jason's here on time, he's dressed up, he opens the door for me, he has a nice family and I'm back before twelve. What more do you want?"

"It's only that—"

"Never mind. You don't want me to be happy!"

"No. No. Of course I want you to be happy. It's just...I don't want you to get hurt."

I want to say something smart. But I don't. Instead, before I can stop myself, I give her a big hug. She holds me tight. I feel like a baby, but all of a sudden I don't care.

Fifteen

I've been skipping Ms. Graham's class big time. For the last couple of weeks I've shown up for attendance, then asked to go to the bathroom and haven't come back. Jason has a spare last period, so we've been taking off to his place to "study."

Today, though, I got narced out by Mr. Carrouthers in

the parking lot. He made me get off Jason's motorcycle and marched me right back to class. "This isn't the first time you've roared off early, is it?" he demanded.

I rolled my eyes. "Oh no? Prove it."

Since Ms. Graham always has me marked present, he can't do anything. But to make sure I don't leave early again, he wants me to report to the office at the end of the day for the next two weeks: otherwise, he's calling home.

Normally, I wouldn't care. But Mom's not stupid. It used to be she'd grill me about boys that didn't exist, but that was just her wanting to be reassured. Lately, she hasn't been asking much of anything. It's as if she suspects what we're up to but is too afraid to know. All the same, if she hears I'm cutting class with Jason, for sure she'll want a "talk" and after that she won't be able to pretend any more. Poor Mom. I can't imagine it. If she finds out I'm having sex *officially* I'll die.

Not that Jason would care.

Forget I said that. That's Katie talking. Jason *does* care; I know he does. He loves me. I mean, he writes me poems and everything. And he's always giving me presents, little surprises like this pinkie ring and a charm bracelet with a big silver J on it. He says the J is a symbol that he's my lucky charm. It's all pretty romantic. Katie should just shut her mouth. What does she know about guys anyway?

Still I wish Jason didn't make such a big deal about sex. Why do we always have to do it? When I ask him, he looks at me all mad. "What's the matter? You frigid? A lesbian, maybe?"

"No," I say. "It's just—couldn't we see a movie instead? This once?" Then he says how I don't love him, and how much he loves me, and how much he needs me, and he keeps going on and on until finally I say, "Okay, I'm sorry. Forget I said anything."

The good news is, despite all the sex I'm not pregnant.

For the first little while, I kept telling myself that each time was going to be the last. But then we'd get together and one thing always led to another. Finally, this one day, I gave up lying to myself and went to the school library before class to check some books about menstrual cycles. I'd thrown out the handout they gave us in health.

Talk about scary. I'm pretty good at math, and counting the days since my last period, I started sweating and panicking, imagining symptoms like crazy. At lunch, I ran out and got one of those tests from the pharmacy. I came back and sat in my bathroom cubicle on the second floor and waited to see if the thingy'd turn color. Was I ever relieved!

That afternoon I tell Jason we've been lucky, but now I'm at my peak and maybe he should use a condom.

He acts shocked. "You mean you're not taking care of that?"

"I can't go to my doctor. I'm too embarrassed. Anyway, a condom's good for other things too. You know, AIDS, VD."

"Are you accusing me of something?"

"No."

"Good. So relax. I'm fine."

But now I'm curious. "Have you been tested?"

"No."

"Then how do you know you're fine?"

"I know." His fists are clenched.

I try to calm him down. "Sorry. I believe you. But we can't take chances. I'm only fifteen. If I get pregnant, they're going to want to know who did it."

"Who says they'd ever have to know you were pregnant? You'd just have to see somebody. My dad knows people." I must look hurt because he snaps, "Fine. Be that way," and fishes for a condom in his underwear drawer, as if I'm really inconveniencing him or something.

When he's in one of those moods, I've learned not to mouth off. So I look at the floor and whisper, "Using a condom doesn't make that much difference, does it?"

Then he gets all tender. He strokes my hair, cups my head in his hands and kisses me gently on the forehead. "It's just that I want to feel close to you."

I feel so guilty. "Me too," I say and kiss him back. "I'll figure something out."

What I figure out is, I can steal pills from Mom for a couple of months. Sneaking them won't be a problem. Mom had almost a year's supply when Dad left and she hasn't used them since. They're at the back of a drawer beside the sink in the bathroom. She's probably forgotten about them, for all I know. For sure she won't remember how many she had.

So that's what I've been doing, with instructions on how to use them courtesy of the Internet access in the school library. Computer class turned out to be useful after all.

Taking the pills makes me feel a lot less paranoid, but I'm still uncomfortable with the sex bit.

At the beginning, I worried his mom would catch us. I'd be like, "Jason, Jason please don't," and he'd be laughing, "Please don't what? Please don't stop?" As it turns out, though, he was right about her: she goes through so much "tomato juice" I hardly think she'd notice if she waltzed right in and sat down beside us.

What gets me is actually "doing it." The kissing part is fine, but that only lasts a minute, and then he's on top of me and I can't even move. I can hardly breathe. A few times I tried to stop him, but I ended up with bruises, and once my blouse got ripped, which took a lot of explaining to Mom.

"I was climbing over a fence at school and it got caught."

"What were you doing climbing over a fence?"

"What do you care?"

"Answer the question."

"Okay, I wasn't climbing over a fence." I rolled my eyes, all sarcastic. "Jason wanted to have sex and he ripped my clothes off. Happy?"

"That isn't funny," Mom said and dropped the subject. It's amazing, but sometimes if you tell the truth, people will act as though they think it's a lie.

I guess it's not *so* bad. At least it's quick. I'm like, "Ow ow ow ow ow," and then Jason makes this groan like he's constipated and says, "That was great," and I go, "Yeah," to keep him happy.

One time I guess I wasn't enthusiastic enough. "All you can say is 'Yeah'?"

That pissed me off. Before I could stop myself, I went, "What do you want? You want me to turn into the school marching band? Do a production number? Light up some fireworks, maybe? Blow the roof off?"

Then he slapped me.

"What was that for?"

"Watch your lip."

That's why I like it better when we get stoned first. Getting stoned doesn't make me paranoid any more. It lets me zone out. I can stare at a point on the ceiling, or the roof of the car, and pretend I'm not there until it's over.

Why am I always complaining? Why am I such a bitch? Jason loves me. I know it, and he says so. Why do I always have to be so negative? I should think of the good stuff—riding on his motorcycle, my charm bracelet.

The other girls keep telling me how lucky I am. Except for Ashley. Last week she said juniors who date seniors are just sex toys, like I'm a whore or something.

"You'd go out with Jason in a flash," I said. "Except he'd never ask you."

"Oh please," she sniffed. "I'm not boy-crazy like you."

"Bullshit," I ripped back. "You stare at guys all the

time when you think no one's looking. And how about your locker, plastered with pictures of Ricky and Leo and whoever?"

"I only put up their pictures because they're talented."

"As if. The only reason you're a virgin is because you've never had a date."

"Well, the only reason you're not *pregnant* is because you're lucky."

"Liar."

"Slut."

I pushed her.

"Girls." It was Mr. Carrouthers. "Is there a problem?"

"No, sir," says Miss Goody-goody.

"Then get to class. Leslie, I'd like a word with you in my office."

What else is new? I glanced at Katie. She was looking at the floor; you'd think someone had died. My insides heaved.

Why does everything go wrong? Why am I such a failure?

Right now I'm looking at Ms. Graham. I'll bet she asks the same things. I wonder if she's ever been in love. I wonder if she's lonely. I wonder if maybe being lonely is better. All I know is, since falling in love with Jason I've been the loneliest of all.

Sixteen

Ms. Graham's gone berserk, and it's only the end of October. Ernie Boulder's lucky he's alive. Mr. Carrouthers is supervising us right now, and for the first time in history, this room is quiet as a morgue.

The class started out pretty ordinary—a lot of bad readers and paper airplanes. We were at the part in the book where Tom is about to get lynched and Scout has the guts to stand up in front of the whole mob—and she's way younger than me!

Anyway, Ms. Graham was going on about how this was one of her favorite scenes, and if everybody would just settle down and listen they'd really enjoy it. Her face was alive, like she meant it, like it mattered—and all of a sudden I got this flash of why she wanted to be a teacher. She actually cares about this stuff.

When I think that, I feel really bad. Caring about something so much it hurts and having everybody else laugh at you—talk about brutal. I pictured Ms. Graham as a teenager with her nose in some book, and the whole school teasing her and being mean. Well, it's thirty years later and nothing has changed. How does she manage to get out of bed in the morning, knowing this is what she's facing?

My head filled with this crazy idea that I should stand on my desk and yell at everyone to shut up. Of course I didn't. I'm not suicidal. But I had the idea all the same.

As per usual, Ernie Boulder was the ringleader. He's discovered he can make himself cross-eyed by touching his tongue to his nose, and he kept turning around to show the card players at the back, who found it majorly hilarious.

"Ernie!" Ms. Graham said. Ernie stopped. Two seconds later he was doing it again. "Ernie!!" Ernie stopped. Two seconds later, the same thing. "Ernie!!!" Well, this went on until nobody was paying any attention to Ms. Graham's favorite scene at all. They were just laughing at Ernie, who was basically daring her to do something.

She did.

Out of the blue, she wheeled to the blackboard, grabbed a yardstick, charged at Ernie and smashed it down. He leaned back just in time. The yardstick broke across his desk. Everyone froze. She could have cracked his head open.

Ms. Graham was pale as chalk. The end of the yardstick fell out of her hand. She teetered there and looked around the room at the silent faces. It was as if she wasn't sure where she was or what had happened. And then this tear slid down her cheek and onto her neck. She didn't say anything, just turned and wobbled out of the room slowly, like a robot.

Things stayed quiet for a very long time. Then someone whispered, "Are you all right?" to Ernie. Unfortunately, he nodded yes. In a few minutes, the talking got louder. Finally, Mr. Carrouthers came in, and everything went silent again. He glared at us: "Get to work, people." Everyone opened their binders and kept their heads down.

Poor Ms. Graham. She didn't mean to lose it. If you ask me, it's a miracle she hasn't attacked someone before. Also a miracle that Ernie's brains aren't splattered all over the ceiling. (It's a good thing it wasn't *me* with that yardstick.)

Lucky for her she missed. Otherwise there'd have been TV crews all over this place, newspaper guys too, and her picture would have been plastered everywhere. Now it'll basically be forgotten, except by our class who saw it. And by Ms. Graham. I bet it'll haunt her till the day she dies.

"There but for the grace of God go I." Katie's started to say that a lot. It's weird hearing it come from somebody under forty, but Katie says she doesn't care. Her church told her it's good to say it when you see somebody homeless or really sick. From now on I'm going to say it whenever I think of Ms. Graham.

Seventeen

Things happening with or without a reason, things we regret—maybe that's why old people lose their minds. Their heads get too full of things they'd rather forget.

I know mine will. There are so many things I've done that make me ashamed. Like never standing up for Ms. Graham. She may be a lousy teacher, but she tries. And how have I thanked her? By bad-mouthing her behind her back and sleeping in the middle of her lessons.

Mom wouldn't do that. She sticks up for people. I re-member buying groceries with her a couple of years back. At the checkout counter, there was a little boy ahead of us with his mother. He took a candy bar from the lowest rack by the cash register. His mother yelled, and he cried, and she started hitting him.

Mom said in a loud voice, "Stop it! What do you think you're doing?" The woman said it was none of Mom's business. Mom said, "Children being hit is everyone's busi-ness." The whole line was staring at us. I was so embar-rassed. But the woman stopped beating on her kid, and afterwards I was proud of Mom for doing it.

That's another thing I feel ashamed about: being so horrible to Mom. I love her. But I sure don't act like I do. I slam my door in her face. I rub it in about Dad leav-ing. Sometimes I feel like I'm mean to everybody who cares about me.

I was worrying about all this when Katie came up to me before school. It's like she has mental telepathy or something.

"I've been thinking over what you said a few weeks back, out by the bleachers," she goes, all serious.

"Katie, please. I didn't mean it."

"No. You're right. I've been so wrapped up in things I've ignored you. I'm sorry."

I don't know what to say, so I nod.

"Anyway," she continues, "I have to get some new tops and I wondered if maybe you want to go shopping with me."

"When?"

"I don't know. Some day after school."

I hesitate. What would I say to Jason? If I don't see him every day he gets in one of his moods. Then I remember he has a dentist appointment coming up. "What about tomorrow afternoon?"

"I have choir practice."

"Oh, right."

I guess I look disappointed, because Katie takes a deep breath. "Okay. Tomorrow. Missing one practice won't hurt."

I'm amazed. For Katie, missing one of her stupid youth groups is almost worse than murder. I'm even more amazed next day when Ashley lays on this guilt trip and Katie says, "Look, Ashley, I go to choir all the time. Missing once isn't the end of the world."

Our trip starts out great: we're playing spy up and down the mall, laughing at all the sales clerks who go on Red Alert when they see a teenager come near their store. We put on lah-de-dah accents, pretending to be rich old people. It's pretty stupid, but it gives us the giggles all the same.

Well, we're having loads of fun until we hit the Gap and start trying on tops. Lots of girls are embarrassed about getting undressed together—after gym, some even change with a towel wrapped around them—but me and Katie have seen each other naked so many times we don't care. We're squashed together in this tiny change room tossing stuff on and off when all of a sudden Katie goes, "Oh my God! What's that on your back?"

I get really scared. I imagine I have this weird growth or something. But when I look in the mirror, all I see is a bruise. It's not hurting or anything. I'd even forgotten I had it.

"Oh, that," I say. "It's nothing."

"It's huge. How did you get it?"

"Who knows? It's *nothing*."

Katie goes really quiet. "It was Jason, wasn't it?"

"No! Look, just because you don't like him doesn't mean he's a wife beater or anything."

"How did it happen, then? It's all big and purple. Don't tell me you can't remember."

"Okay, if it makes you happier, I fell backwards and hit my back on a doorknob."

"Nobody falls backwards unless they're pushed."

"Quit with the Nancy Drew crap."

"I'll quit when you tell me who pushed you."

"It wasn't a push. Anyway, it was my fault. I was being mouthy and Jason just accidentally sort of bumped into me."

"Oh my God! What if you'd hit your spine? What if you'd broken your back?"

"Well, I didn't. Don't be so dramatic. It's only been once, anyway, and if you tell anyone—"

"What about those marks on your arms?"

"No big deal."

"Is this why you haven't been coming to gym?"

She's got me. I don't like getting hit, even if it's only been a couple of times and even if it's to teach me a lesson, like Jason says, but even worse is the idea that other people might find out. They wouldn't understand. So I've been hiding my bruises with long-sleeved sweaters and jeans, which I've started to wear anyhow, on account of Jason doesn't like other guys staring at me. I also stopped going to gym. (Apparently Ms. Patrick thinks cramps can go on forever. Personal experience, no doubt.)

"I just bruise easy, that's all," I shrug.

"You do not. Leslie, you've got to stop going out with him."

I grab her by the elbows and stare into her eyes. "Mind your own business. Stuff between me and Jason is private. Okay?"

"You're getting beat up."

"I am not!" And I give her my hardest, hardest look. "Besides, aren't you supposed to be the big Christian? Whatever happened to forgive and forget?"

"This is different."

"It is not. Now swear you'll never blab to anyone." Her eyes are big and pleading, but no way I'm taking no for an answer. "Katie, if you don't swear, I'll never speak to you again. I mean it."

She bites her lip. "Okay," she says softly. She's almost crying. "But is it all right if I pray for you?"

"Fine. If it makes you feel better. Just don't tell me about it or I'll barf."

For the next few days, Katie keeps coming up to me all soulful and whispering, "Are you okay?" It's pretty creepy.

What a dumb question. Of course I'm not okay. But then I've never been okay. What's okay, anyway? I bet it doesn't even exist.

Life sucks. I want it to end.

Eighteen

It's one o'clock in the morning, and I'm in my room writing this down because if I don't I will never get to sleep. I may not get to sleep anyway, but if it's all out on paper I'll be able to see it and maybe it won't keep running around in my head driving me crazy.

I am in unbelievably deep shit.

The thing is, somebody's read my journal—my supposedly *private* journal—and her name is Ms. Tracey James. She knows everything, all about Jason and me having sex, and me getting hit, and Mom and Dad and Dad's slutty girlfriend Brenda. Plus what I wrote about Mr. Carrouthers and Ms. Graham and Katie's mom and God only knows what else.

Even worse, Ms. James has given my journal to the principal, and I have to go with her to the office first thing tomorrow morning. (It was supposed to be after school today, but I threw up, so they let me go home.)

All tonight I sat by the phone, so if the principal called I could intercept and say Mom was out of town (forever).

But she never called, which is actually worse, because now the suspense is killing me.

At first, I thought I'd phone the school tomorrow pretending to be Mom and say I was sick. Then I could basically wait for things to blow over. But the secretaries know my voice, and they also have Mom's work number. Besides, my only chance for Mom not to hear about my journal is for me to see the principal and beg her to keep things quiet. I mean, I'll do detentions for the rest of my life if it keeps Mom from finding out what I've been up to.

And then there's Jason. So far he doesn't know about my journal. At least, I don't think he does. But if the school makes a big deal about it and he ends up in trouble, who knows what he'll do?

Ms. James arrived a week ago, the last week of October. She's taking over from Ms. Graham, who won't be back until at least after Christmas. (Make that Christmas a couple of hundred years from now.)

Ms. James is under thirty and looks like she used to be a Cute and Perky, except for now she's organized and scary. Like when she's introducing herself, Ernie Boulder makes a fart sound with his armpit. Ms. Graham would've gotten flustered and the card players would've gone berserk. But Ms. James just glances at the seating plan and eyeballs Ernie with a look that could stop a truck.

Everyone freezes to see what she'll do. Then, right when we can't stand it any more, she says in this crisp voice, "Ernie, we're going to be seeing a lot of each other over the next few months. This experience can be either pleasant or unpleasant. It's your choice. What's it to be?"

Ernie shrinks into his desk.

"I beg your pardon?"

"Pleasant," he whispers.

Ms. James eyeballs him for another five seconds, then looks at the rest of us. "Are we all understood?" A pause. We stare at our desks, except for the card players, who are quietly hiding their deck. When they're finished, Ms. James tilts her eyebrow. "Good."

We breathe a sigh of relief.

"As for your mid-term reports, due at the end of next week: I will be entering your grades for English once I receive a copy of your marks from Ms. Graham." Nobody's talking, but we're giving each other looks. "What seems to be the problem?"

We all sit tight, except for Cindy Williams, who starts flapping her arm like a seagull. "But Ms. James, we haven't *had* any marks."

"What do you mean, you haven't had any marks?"

"Ms. Graham never gave any tests or essays or anything, except for a content quiz and these question and answer sheets she never collected." Here Cindy shows off her binder, knowing the rest of ours are empty.

Does Ms. James panic? No way. If that's the case, she says, tomorrow we'll start with a test on *Mockingbird,* followed by an in-class essay, with automatic zeros to anyone missing without a doctor's note.

"But we haven't finished reading it," cries someone from the back.

"Then you'll have a busy night."

She got our tests and essays back to us within two days, which should put her in the speed category of the Guinness Book of World Records. All the same, I only realized how big a marking maniac she is this afternoon. At the end of the period, she says she'd like to see me privately. Once we're alone, she tells me it's no secret she needs marks for our reports, so she's started to grade our journals.

"You're reading them?"

"Yes. And as you might guess, I find yours very disturbing."

"You have no right!" I blurt out. "Ms. Graham promised they'd be private!"

"I'm sorry. I didn't know." She pauses. "Leslie, do you understand the meaning of physical assault? Sexual assault? Rape?"

I have a hard time breathing. "Yeah. So? What's that got to do with me?"

"It's what you wrote about."

"It is not." I struggle to my feet. "That journal is my property. Where is it? Give it back!" I try to look tough, but I'm shaky.

Ms. James stays calm. She's not mad, just very serious. "I'm afraid I can't."

"Yes, you can! Give it back or else!"

"Leslie, I have a legal and a moral obligation to report

abuse. I've given your journal to the principal. After this discussion, she wants to see us in her office."

"No!" I sink back into my seat. And then a horrible thought, a sick feeling in the pit of my stomach. "What's going to happen to Jason?"

"The important question is what's happening to you." Ms. James's voice is kind, but I hate her like I've never hated anyone before. "Leslie, you've been hurt. You need help."

"Forget about me. What's going to happen to Jason?"

"You'll have to talk to Ms. Barker about it."

And that's when I threw up.

Nineteen

At our school, retired principals get places like the gym or the library named after them. I have the perfect spot to name for Ms. Barker: the office washroom. I can just picture this little plaque over the paper dispenser: "The Stella Barker Memorial Problem Solver."

Ms. Stella Barker. I call her Beachball.

I don't call her Beachball because she's all puffed up—which she is on account of I bet she likes to drink. No, I call her Beachball because she rolls whichever way the wind is blowing. If it's convenient to say, "The grass is green," that's what she'll say. But if tomorrow it's convenient to say, "The grass is blue," well, she'll say that too. She calls it being "flexible." I call it being a weasel.

For instance, last year there was this math test that by some miracle Cindy Williams forgot to study for. The minute Cindy saw Mr. Kogawa handing out the questions, she had a panic attack and took off.

Naturally, Mr. Kogawa gave her a zero. But Cindy got all teary, said she'd been sick. He didn't buy it, because he'd seen her goofing around right before class. So Cindy went whining to her mother, who complained to Beachball that this zero would wreck Cindy's straight As.

Did Beachball side with Mr. Kogawa? No way. Cindy's mom is on the Parents' Council, so Beachball made the zero disappear, and Kogawa ended up looking like a fool. Cindy bragged all over that her mother told Beachball, "Either you deal with Fred Kogawa, or I go to the school board." Personally, if I was Cindy, I wouldn't brag about being a suck but, hey, whatever makes you feel important.

Anyway, two weeks later, I missed a geography test because Mom's alarm clock didn't go off. I got a zero too. So, I figured, no sweat, I'll do like Cindy's mom and talk to Beachball. But surprise, surprise: when I saw her in the hall, she wouldn't even discuss it.

Beachball likes to tell parents that she "addresses individual student needs." Hah! She just plays favorites. That's why she can't stand Mr. Carrouthers. He hands out suspensions no matter who your parents are. He's sort of an equal opportunity hard-ass. Beachball could care less if kids like me fail or get suspended. But kids whose parents can make trouble, that's another story.

Since Carrouthers doesn't care about pushy parents, he makes headaches for Beachball. As a result, she bad-mouths him out loud to teachers in the corridor and tells her little pets they don't have to show up for his detentions.

Last year when Carrouthers called Mom about my "absences," I asked how come she listens to him when the principal doesn't. Mom was shocked when I told her some of the things I've heard Beachball say. But she wasn't shocked at Beachball. No, she was shocked at *me* for telling "lies." According to her, Ms. Barker would never be so unprofessional. But she is. Ask anybody. She's a bitch with dimples. Ashley A-hole grown up.

Carrouthers may be a jerk, but at least he's a jerk to everyone. With him you know where you stand. The line is clear. But with Beachball, forget it. Logic and fairness are out the window.

That's why I'm scared about this meeting. There's no way to figure out what she'll do. Beachball might feel sorry for me and pretend nothing's happened. On the other hand, she might call Mom and try to get me locked up.

Yeah, locked up. Last year, after I entered this "phase" I'm supposedly going through, Beachball invited Mom and me to her office. (Carrouthers had suspended me after I got nailed for forging Mom's signature on a school letter home.) Beachball gave Mom a coffee and put on this caring routine, but what she really wanted was to get me tranked.

"We've found that students with hyperactivity, like

Leslie, have benefited from Ritalin," she announced, as if she's a psychiatrist or something.

Lucky for me, Mom grew up in a small town. Even *talk* about drugs scares her. "I'd be a little uncomfortable putting Leslie on medication," she frowned.

"Hey, I'm sitting right here," I wanted to scream. I just love it when you're the topic of conversation and adults act like you're not even there.

"These days medication is quite commonplace," Beachball went on. "To tell you the truth," and here she gave a little laugh, "half my staff are on antidepressants." She meant that as a joke, but it wouldn't surprise me, the way she runs things.

"Well, it's something to think about," Mom said.

So on top of everything else, I can't help but worry that maybe this time Beachball will go for broke and try to get me committed. Especially since Ms. James says I need help. With Beachball, anything's possible.

Twenty

Beachball doesn't get up when we enter her office. She motions for us to sit down, then pulls my journal from the piles of paper on her desk and flicks it in front of me.

Silence.

She purses her lips like they're a pair of sugar tongs. "I must say you have quite a lively prose style." She makes a kind of grimace. I guess this is one of those jokes you're not supposed to laugh at. "You have scribbled any number of accusations," she continues, "allegations that could destroy a young man's life."

"No one was supposed to read my journal," I say, staring at the edge of her desk. "It was supposed to be private."

"Is that so?" Out of the corner of my eye, I see Beachball shoot a look at Ms. James.

"Please don't tell my mom."

"Your journal leaves us no choice but to tell your mother. And the child welfare authorities. And the police."

"The *police?*"

"They will need to make a full criminal investigation. You should know that the McCreadys are unlikely to take these charges lightly. They may well lay charges of their own."

"But the journal's a lie!" I blurt out. "All that never happened! I made it up!" My head is full of Mom collapsing, Jason in jail, me charged with something. The world is coming to an end.

"So this is a fabrication?"

"Yes."

"It most certainly is not!" Ms. James interrupts.

"Says who?" I yell at her. "Who made you God?"

"Leslie, if you don't tell the truth, we can't help you."

"According to Leslie, she doesn't need help," Beachball snaps. "What she needs is to have her privacy respected."

Ms. James looks as if she's been sideswiped by a truck.

Beachball turns to me with a tight smile. "Might I suggest that in future you take more care with what you write. Might I further suggest, if you wish to avoid this fantasy becoming reality, you comport yourself with more discretion."

Ms. James goes ballistic. "Ms. Barker, surely you aren't suggesting that it's acceptable for people to hurt other people because of how they act."

Beachball's eyes narrow. "I'm afraid you haven't heard what I said."

"Maybe not, but I heard what you meant."

"I'm sorry you choose to misinterpret. In any case, this matter is no longer your concern."

It's like a Ping-Pong game, with me as the ball. I just want to get out of here. "So can I please have my journal back?"

Beachball puffs herself up all grand. "You may. And I trust you will know what to do with it. Libel, defamation and slander are serious offences."

"You can't mean this is the end of it," Ms. James gasps.

Beachball pauses. "Close the door on your way out, would you, Leslie? I'd like to have a word with Ms. James." The last thing I hear before the door shuts is Beachball spitting, "You know, Tracey, in my experience, insubordination is not the best route to a long and happy career."

I put my journal in my bag and head to my locker. No way am I going back to class. I slump on the floor. Next thing I know, I'm staring at somebody's feet. I look up. It's Ms. James.

"Leslie," she says, "I want you to know, if you ever need help, I'm here."

I am so furious at her for putting me through this. All the same, part of me wants to thank her. But if I did, I'd cry. So instead I just say, "Whatever."

Twenty-one

After Ms. James leaves, I stay by my locker worrying. How much should I tell Jason about what's going on? Maybe I should pretend this morning never happened. But there's always spies around, and I could have been seen in the office by kids going to the washroom, wandering the halls, you name it. Gossip could already be flying around. If Jason hears anything, I could say I was taking the home-room attendance down to the office or signing in late. But if someone actually saw me going through Beachball's door, he'll be on my case big time.

I don't get why Jason always has to know what I'm doing. He says I don't have to get it, it's just a fact. Since I'm his girl, he has a right to know everything. It's no use arguing, unless I want to get him mad. Besides, when he does explain, the reason he gives is always the same. According to him, it's because he loves me and worries about losing me.

"But if you love me, why can't you trust me?"

"I do. I don't trust other guys, that's all. They want to get into your pants, you know."

"That's their problem. I'm not interested in anyone else."

"So if you're not interested, you've got nothing to hide. Hey, what's the matter, don't *you* trust *me?*"

When he puts it like that, I get mixed up. Then he holds me and snuggles me into his chest and kisses my hair and tells me, "I need to protect you. If I don't know what you're doing and you get into trouble, how can I look after you? I'd never forgive myself if you got hurt and I wasn't there."

"Right. I'm sorry." It's not exactly what I'm thinking, but I'm too confused to say anything else, and besides, I don't want another bruise. Jason has no idea how strong he is when he grabs me, which is what he does when he wants to make a point. He's always making points.

So figuring what to tell him about my meeting with Beachball is really tricky. If I try to hide it, for sure I'll act paranoid and he'll sense something's wrong. But if I tell him the truth, he'll go bananas.

In the end, I don't have to decide. Right before the period ends, he whips around the corner out of the blue. "Get up. We're going outside."

"Sure. I just gotta straighten up my locker."

He slams my locker door shut so hard it bounces back open and a couple of books fall out. "Is that straight enough?" He yanks me to my feet.

"Ow. What's with you?"

"Shut up."

I barely have time to grab my bag before he's hauling me down the hall by my elbow. A teacher sticks his head out of class to see what's going on. Jason drops my arm, but we keep moving.

"Sorry," I say to the teacher as we whisk by. "We're just going to the library."

Jason is walking so fast it's hard to keep up. But I know better than to fall behind. We're heading towards the south exit at the far end, away from the street, where the school hides its dumpsters. Nobody ever goes down there on account of it's all storage rooms, and once you step outside the door locks behind you. Basically the area's deserted except for late-night parties. In the mornings, the janitors have to check the alcove for needles, condoms and smashed beer bottles.

He kicks the door open and pushes me outside. "Okay, bitch, you got something to tell me?"

I try to stall. "What are you talking about?"

"Don't play games," he snarls. He bounces me off the wall. "What did you tell her?"

"Who?"

He makes a fist. "Barker. Don't play games."

"She called me in for skipping." I stumble backward towards the dumpsters.

"This is your last chance, bitch. What'd you tell her?" He grabs an old chunk of paving stone.

"No. Stop!" I trip. I scrape my hand on the gravel. I try

crawling away on my right arm, shielding my head with my left. "Ms. James read my journal."

"What journal?"

"The one I've been doing in English."

"You wrote about me?"

"It wasn't supposed to get read."

"Answer the question." He squeezes the stone.

"Yes."

"Bitch!" He whips it over my head. It clangs off the dumpster.

"I'm sorry. I'm sorry!"

Jason rages towards me, his face all twisted. Oh God, help! I scrunch into a ball. He jumps on top, yanks my arms down, pins me.

"Get off me. Ow!"

"What did you write?"

"Just stuff."

"What stuff?" He knees my ribs.

"Leave me alone!"

"What stuff?"

"Nothing. Just stupid stuff."

He's right in my face now, talking hot and low. He's sweating like mad. "Well, that's real interesting. Because I had a talk with Barker too."

"What?"

"She called me in. Said there'd been a complaint. No names, but we all know who, don't we?"

"I didn't complain."

"Said I better be careful how I treat 'young women,' how I wouldn't want to get misinterpreted. What'd she mean by that?" He squeezes his knee in my gut.

"I don't know. Ow. You're crushing. Someone's gonna see us."

"Big deal. You fell. You hurt yourself. I'm helping you up." He jerks me to my feet. "Last chance. What'd you write?"

Suddenly I don't care what happens. "I wrote what you do to me."

For a second, Jason goes calm. He chuckles, shakes his head and turns away. Then, before I know what hit me, he hauls off and smashes my shoulder. I crash back against the dumpster, crack my head, slide down into a heap.

"Where's your journal now?"

"In Barker's office," I lie.

"Get it back. I want it burned."

"I can't."

He boots the dumpster, to the right of my face.

Words spill out of my mouth. "I hate you! You're a pig! A pig! You're just like Katie said!"

"And you're a slut. A piece of toilet paper." He boots the dumpster again, closer.

"Go ahead. Kick me in the head. Kick me where people will see the bruise. Smash my face. Break my jaw. Why don't you, coward?" I can hardly believe what I'm saying. "You and me, we're finished."

"Oh, yeah? We're finished when I say we're finished."

"No. We're finished when *I* say. And I say *now*. It's over. O.V.E.R."

I expect him to go crazy, but instead he laughs. "Hey, the bitch can spell. I wonder if she can spell 'Polaroid.'"

"What do you mean?"

"I'm talking about the Polaroids I took on our first night, when you were passed out. I think your mother'd like to see the kind of slut she raised. Pretty flexible. I'm surprised you didn't make cheerleader."

"You're lying."

"You don't want to find out," he taunts.

He kicks some gravel at my face, then turns away. As he saunters off, he calls back over his shoulder, "I'll be in the parking lot at three-thirty. Don't keep me waiting."

Twenty-two

The books that fell out of my locker are probably being kicked up the hall by people changing classes. But that's all happening on another planet. I've only got one thing to think about besides throwing up, and that's getting to Jason's. Now. While he's out. If there are Polaroids, they're in his room, and I'm getting them back. Maybe they don't even exist, but I can't take the chance.

I leave the school grounds as fast as I can. I grab a bus to the subway, take the subway to Sherwood station, then get another bus to Jason's subdivision. Walking up his street, I feel like an alien. I imagine all these rich housewives and nannies watching me out of their living room windows, getting ready to call the police.

Nobody walks around here. Even if they wanted to, there're no sidewalks, just curbs. Around here walking is next to a crime. You're expected to be rich enough to drive a car. If you're not, you must be casing houses to loot.

Especially if you look like me. My jeans are ripped from the gravel. I'm covered in scrapes, my hair is a mess, and I've got a bump on the back of my head that feels like a watermelon. What'll I say when I see Jason's mother? "Hello, Mrs. McCready, your son is an asshole, but hey, don't worry, have another drink"?

When I get to his house, her Camry's not there. Is she out, or just upstairs comatose, the car in the garage? I check my watch. It's not quite noon. I can't believe she's out already; Jason told me she sometimes sleeps all day.

I ring the doorbell. It's one of those little chimes that are supposed to sound elegant but just sound phony, the kind they have at fancy shoe stores. No answer. I ring it again. Still nothing. Time for drastic action—I grab the brass door knocker, which weighs a ton, and bang away for all I'm worth.

Silence.

I can't just leave. Not without what I came for. But by now I'm sure I've got the whole neighborhood staring at me. If I try to break in, they'll call the police for sure.

Suddenly I get this wild idea. I wave at the empty living room window, like there's somebody inside, then say in a loud voice, "Oh hi, Mrs. McCready. You want me to meet you in the garage? Okay."

What, am I crazy? Like that's supposed to fool anybody?

I want to run. But I can't. Not now. The garage door lock has been broken since Jason gave it a boot a month ago. I raise the door a bit, slip inside and close it behind me.

I know the hiding place for the house key is under the watering can by the garbage pail. Why do they even *have* a watering can? As if Mrs. McCready would be caught dead holding one. And as for the mister, he's never home long enough to water.

I let myself in. The warning from their alarm system starts beeping, but that's okay. Before the alarm goes off, I punch in the code and disarm it. I've seen Jason punch it so often, I know it by heart. 8-7-4-2, the last four digits of their phone number. What a stupid code. Like, do they *want* to get robbed?

Okay. I'm inside. The alarm is turned off. So far so good. I take a deep breath. I tell myself to relax. If the neighbors are nosy they'll have seen me around here before; they'll just go back to their cleaning or watching TV.

All the same, for a second, I'm afraid to move. Even though there's nobody around to hear me, I'm terrified of making a sound. It's as if I think the furniture is alive, listening for intruders. How do guys rob places for a living? Aren't they afraid of giving themselves heart attacks?

I have a flash that maybe I'm not alone, that Mrs. McCready really *is* here, that she didn't hear me because she's downstairs working out on the Thighmaster. "Mrs. McCready?" I call out. "It's me. Leslie."

Only silence. I don't know how much time I have. I better move fast.

I'm thinking very clearly now: if I were Jason, where would I hide my porn? I'd want it where my mom and dad wouldn't stumble across it and where I'd have easy access for when I wanted to play with myself. Guessing that's what he uses the pictures for makes me feel dirty, but I'm realistic. I run upstairs to his bedroom. Now what? I figure his porn will be all in one place, because every extra hiding spot's an extra chance to get caught.

I check under the rugs, under his bed, between his box spring and mattress. I check his closet, his clothes drawers, the back of his sweater shelves. Nothing.

On the closet floor, behind his shoes, is a row of cardboard boxes and an old tackle box. I open the big boxes first: just junk, old kids' toys, ratty sneakers. Next the tackle box. I expect to see lures and fish hooks, but instead there are birthday and Christmas cards from when Jason was little.

The phone rings. My heart stops. It rings again, then silence. Either they've hung up or the voice mail's kicked in. I hold my breath as if somehow the person who's calling could hear me. But that's too weird. And my search is taking too long. I panic back into action.

I race to Jason's bookcase. I empty it, shake each book

fast, hoping the pictures'll fall out. I yank out his desk draw-ers, turn them upside down. I rip his posters off the wall. Nothing. Maybe he was bluffing. Oh my God. His room is a mess, but I can't take time to put things back. I've commit-ted a B&E. Again, I imagine police. I've got to take off.

My legs start running. They fly downstairs. They're about to race me out the front door when suddenly I stop in my tracks. There's something not right about the Christmas cards in that tackle box.

I run back upstairs. I grab the tackle box out of the closet. Turn it over. Out fall the cards. And a manila enve-lope, folded over and held shut with a thick elastic. I know what I'll find before I open it.

Under the six Polaroids of me are some of two girls I've never seen before. These girls aren't in the downstairs rec room. They're someplace else. One of them isn't even in a house. She's outside, at what looks like the end of an old woods road with bushes and trees and weird shadows all around. It's night, and the light's coming from in front of her. I'll bet it's from the headlights of Jason's mom's car.

There's something familiar about these pictures. The way we look. Our age. Our hair. The way we're posed.

A sound fills the room, a kind of moan-roar coming from inside me. I start to rock. But I can't lose it now. I stuff the pictures back into the envelope, stash it in my bag, get to my feet, stagger down the hall to the top of the stairs.

I can hardly see. But I can hear all right. And what I hear is the front door opening.

Twenty-three

I duck into the master bedroom, the nearest room available. Downstairs, the front door closes. Whoever's there puts something heavy on the floor.

"Jason?" It's Mrs. McCready. "Jason, are you home?" A pause. "That's strange."

What's she talking about? Of course. There's no alarm warning. I turned it off. Now what should I do: stay put or come out and hope for the best?

Just as I'm about to give myself up, I hear the sound of cans clattering and Mrs. McCready humming her way to the kitchen. Groceries. If she's gone to unpack them, she's not upset; she must figure she forgot to set the alarm when she left.

I hear cans hitting the counter. Good. If I slip downstairs real quiet, maybe I can make it out the front door before she's finished. After all, it's a new house with no creaks, carpet everywhere.

I step out into the upstairs hall. But I can see the back of her legs heading into the living room. What a break! She didn't glance upstairs. I retreat inside the bedroom door and stand stock-still, listening for clues about what to do next.

From downstairs, I hear someone talking. Mrs. McCready's listening to her voice mail on the speaker phone. And then . . . humming. And it's coming upstairs!

Should I run to the ensuite bathroom? But what if she has to pee? I can hide behind the shower curtain. But there isn't one; it's made of glass. At the last minute, I dive under the bed. I can see what's happening from a crack between the floor and where the eiderdown ends.

Flash. The door to Jason's room is open. What if she sees the mess?

But she isn't paying attention. She comes into the room. She's walking towards me. She stops, turns and sits on the edge of the bed.

For a few minutes, she sits very still. I hear a gentle clink of ice cubes. She must be having a "tomato juice." I hear her set the glass down on the night table and sigh.

All this time, I'm staring at the back of her high heels. It's weird. I'm having palpitations, but all I can think is, She wears high heels shopping? And now she slips them off. She stands up, walks to the closet and unzips her dress. She hangs it up and comes back to the bed in her bra and panties. She crawls under the eiderdown.

Oh no. She's taking a nap.

Out of nowhere, I remember this time when I was a kid. Mom took me to her dentist appointment; I guess she couldn't find a babysitter or something. While she was having a filling done, I hung out in the waiting room. For some reason the receptionist had to step out, leaving me all alone with my coloring book, when all of a sudden in walked this blind man. I'd never seen a blind person up close before, but I could tell on account of his white cane.

"Hello?" the man said.

Silence. I remember thinking maybe I should say something, but I was kind of scared because I was only six and he was a grownup, so I just sat there.

The man tapped his cane to the chair right across from me and sat down. He stared like he could see me, but of course he couldn't. I was invisible.

For a while, it was kind of exciting. It was like a game where I had magical powers. But pretty soon it started to get creepy. Every so often the man would tilt his head as if he was listening, as if he knew I was there. I wanted to say something, but now I was afraid to get caught. Then the receptionist came back in, and while she took his information I tiptoed out to the hall.

I'm even more creeped out now, lying under the bed with Mrs. McCready trying to sleep over top of me. Only there's no receptionist to rescue me this time. And the longer I lie here, the more I worry about Jason. What's going to happen if he comes home?

Lucky for me, Mrs. McCready can't sleep. Within ten minutes she's flopping around, rolling over and over like a dog doing tricks. Then she lets rip a big ripe fart. I'm so amazed I don't know whether to gag or laugh.

"Lord," she mutters and gets up. I watch her put on her bathrobe, walk out of the room and head towards the stairs. I wait just long enough to make sure she's really gone, and then I crawl out of hiding. I peek into the hall. The coast is clear. I tiptoe to the top of the stairs. I listen hard. No sound.

Here goes nothing.

I race down the stairs as fast as I can—and run right into Mrs. McCready at the bottom.

She screams. Her left hand is clutched to her throat. Her right hand is clutched around another glass of tomato juice. "Leslie!"

"Mrs. McCready!"

"What are you doing here?"

"School's out early. Jason said to come by."

"He's here?"

"No. He dropped me off. But he should be back soon. He's doing an errand."

She looks fuzzy. "How long have you been here?"

"I'm not sure."

Then it's like she sees me for the first time. "My God, Leslie, you're a mess."

"Am I?"

"Are you all right?"

I fake a laugh. "Oh, you mean my clothes and stuff. Today, at school, it was Hobo Day."

"Hobo Day?"

Talk about dumb. But I can't back out now. "We were supposed to come dressed like tramps. Student Council thought it'd be great for school spirit. We had to bring cans of food, too, for these boxes in the lobby that we're donating to the Food Bank. I brought a can of spaghetti."

Mrs. McCready considers this. "What a wonderful idea." Thank God she's drunk.

"Yeah. It was lots of fun. But I better get going. I just remembered Mom needs me home to help her clean up. She's having friends over for bridge."

"Why don't you wait till Jason gets back? He can give you a ride."

"That's okay. I can take the bus. I don't want to be a drag."

"Don't be silly."

"No, really. It's no big deal."

"Well, suit yourself." Mrs. McCready passes a hand vaguely across her forehead. She's looking into the air now, at a point somewhere way behind the middle of my forehead.

For a split second, I imagine she's somebody else. She's still elegant, even in a yellow chenille bathrobe, all limbs and high cheekbones. But I can see pale scars along her ears, and instead of looking young, she looks bizarre. Her eyebrows are all plucked and painted, which makes her appear sort of surprised.

I must be hallucinating, because she doesn't look like herself any more. She looks like Ms. Graham. Ms. Graham with all the fat sucked out of her. Ms. Graham if she didn't have to worry about having a job. Ms. Graham all bewildered and too afraid to think or do anything.

Check please.

I wave like a maniac. "See you later," I babble. I scramble out the door while I still have a brain.

Twenty-four

All the way to the bus stop, I'm scared I'll bump into Jason. It's barely two o'clock. He should still be at school, but what if he's skipping? I keep an eye open for escape routes. If worst comes to worst, I figure I can cut across backyards. He wouldn't be able to follow on his motorcycle. But what if I meet a pit bull? Or somebody raking leaves?

I want to be home under the covers. But no way for that. The minute Jason sees his room, he's going to freak and come after me. I picture me trapped in the apartment, with him in the hall trying to break down the door. Or the cops coming to arrest me after Mrs. McCready sees the chaos. No. Home isn't safe.

Besides, I can't go there with these Polaroids. Not till I think of a hiding place. I want to rip them up, but I'm not stupid. If the cops really do come for me, the pictures are all I have to stop the McCreadys from pressing charges. Not that I'd ever hand them over, of course, but I could make the threat. Would that count as blackmail?

All these thoughts zap my brain as I ride the bus to the subway. Once I'm at the station, inside, underground, I start to relax. If cops are after me, they won't look here. And Jason can't ride his bike down the escalator. Even if he did, what could he do to me in front of all these people?

As long as I stay where I am, I'll be fine. I buy an Oh Henry bar at the kiosk and sit on a bench to eat it, watching people get on and off the trains.

I wonder how long I could live here. I picture me holed up in a cardboard box somewhere down the tunnel, coming out early in the morning to stock up on Coke, potato chips, hot dogs and cheese nachos. I'd have to watch out for security cops and people who might have seen my picture on a milk carton once I'm reported missing. But it wouldn't be bad, apart from the rats and finding a bathroom: the subway toilets have been locked up for years.

Of course, Mom would be worried. But I could use the pay phone to leave a nice message on the answering machine saying I'm okay and I love her.

Just as I polish off my bar and get ready to toss the wrapper, I see these two subway patrol cops. They look pretty grisly, like they don't get out much. They start to walk towards me. What do they want?

I stare at the wad of gum squashed on the floor in front of me. If I stare hard enough, maybe I'll disappear. It works. The cops walk right past me and start hassling this guy playing guitar at the end of the platform. They're just like Mr. Carrouthers, only without teachers' college.

When the train pulls in, I hop on. It's pretty full, so I shuffle to the end of the car and find an inside seat. My back is protected. But not my mind. Within a few minutes, it starts playing tricks. I imagine somebody's going to steal my bag and find the Polaroids, put them on the Internet. I break into a cold sweat and wrap my arms through the bag's shoulder straps.

Then I wonder if being paranoid makes me seem suspicious. Do I look like a drug dealer protecting my stash? I concentrate on acting normal. But the more I concentrate on that, the more I want to freak.

You can't freak forever, though; it takes too much energy. Without knowing when it happens, I zone out, bored, staring out the window at the tunnel and the stations flying by, until I'm sort of hypnotized. I stay like a zombie for I don't know how long, and then my mind starts kicking back in.

I think about how if I didn't look at my watch I wouldn't know what time it is. So much has happened since this morning in Beachball's office. I mean, that could be years ago.

Time is just plain weird. When I was seven in Seattle, my Granny P. and Annie Wilson were at the center of my life. Now that Granny's dead, I only remember her in flashes, like snapshots, and Annie could be anywhere. It's like time keeps ticking, adding new people and things until sooner or later everybody forgets all about the old ones, even the old ones they used to care about.

I wish time was something I could grab hold of. I wish I could stop it from moving and making good things disappear. On the plus side, though, it makes bad things go away too. Maybe it'll help me get over this nightmare called Jason.

Before every test, Katie likes to say, "This too shall pass." Actually, what she says is, "This too shall pass. Even if we don't." Mom has a favorite saying a lot the same: "Time heals all wounds." What with all the Dad stuff, I wonder if she still believes it. I don't. Time makes things go away, but it doesn't heal: it's more like an anesthetic.

I check the other passengers. Nobody's looking my way. They're all looking straight ahead, brain dead. It's like they walked in, sat down and went from Technicolor to gray. I'm in a train full of robots.

This idea makes me smile for the next three stops. Then I start obsessing about Jason again. It's like that for the next couple of hours. I go from scared to bored to giddy and back again as I sit there riding the subway back and forth across the city.

Finally, I start getting lonely, too.

I check my watch. It's almost five. Jason will have left school ages ago. Has he seen his room? What's he doing?

I get off at the stop near Katie's and call her from the pay phone.

"Hi, it's Leslie." I hear pots and pans and a bunch of people laughing.

"Are you okay? Where *were* you this aft? I locked up your locker. It was a mess."

"Katie, I have to talk to you."

"My aunt and uncle are visiting from out of town. We're having a reunion. I'm supposed to entertain my little cousin."

"This is an emergency."

In the background, Mrs. Kincaid is saying, "Katie, get off the phone. We're expecting a call from Janice, and Chloe wants to play Ping-Pong."

"Okay," Katie calls out, then whispers, "I gotta go. I'll call you back later."

"I'm not at home. I'm not safe. I'm—look, if you don't see me again, it's because I may be dead."

"*What?*"

"I mean it."

"Where are you? Call the police. No, wait, *I'll* call the police."

"Call the police and I'll kill myself. Katie, I'm in so much trouble."

"Look, don't cry. Come over right away. We'll—I don't know, but we'll figure out something."

Twenty-five

When I get there, Katie's out front on the sidewalk watching her cousin Chloe play hopscotch. I'm pretty sure this is so I won't have to ring the doorbell and get intercepted by her mom.

Chloe looks like a glass of skim milk, all scrubbed and polished like she's going to church. Your basic trophy kid. The kind parents show off to make other parents jealous. I almost feel sorry for her. Instead of friends, I'll bet all she has is a bunch of stuffed animals. I picture her playing house with them, all alone in a cheery antiseptic bedroom plastered with Disney characters.

At the sight of me her lip quivers and her eyebrows do the Wave.

"It's okay, Chloe," Katie says. "This is my friend Leslie. Why don't you go down to the basement and watch cartoons?"

Chloe does what she's told. Fast.

"Leslie! You look awful!"

"No shit, Sherlock." I tell her about the journal and Ms. James and Beachball and how me and Jason have broken up.

Katie's all excited. I know she wants to jump up and down, but these days she's making a big effort not to be so immature. She needs to work harder. This time, she shouts "*Great!*" at the top of her lungs.

"Don't." I shoot her a look. "I mean it. If you tell me God's answered your prayers, I swear I'll punch you."

"I'm sorry. Only I've been so worried."

"I know. Thanks. But here's the worst." I tell her about the pictures. I don't want to, but I can't help myself. I can't hold it in. Besides, she never blabbed about me getting hit.

Most of the girls at school would act shocked and give me a lecture. Then they'd ask to see the pictures for themselves. They'd pretend it was out of being a friend and wanting to share the horror, but really it'd be so they could act even more shocked and then run around telling everybody.

But not Katie. She gets very quiet and then hugs me.

That's when the Wicked Witch of the West comes out. "Oh, hello, Leslie," she says, not even pretending to smile. "May I have a word with you, Katie?" Before Katie has time to get to the porch, her mom starts in. "Poor Chloe's sitting downstairs all by herself in front of the television set. Tell Leslie you'll see her some other time."

"But Mom—" Katie whispers urgently in her ear.

"That's nothing to joke about."

"I'm not."

"Fine. Ten minutes." She glares in my direction and disappears.

I want to die. "You told her?"

"Of course not. I said you were thinking of making a decision for the Lord."

"You told her *what?*" I see myself in a white robe getting dunked in ice-cold water in the baptismal tub at Katie's church.

"Never mind. Let's get out of here. I'll tell her I was so busy hearing your witness I forgot about the time."

"She won't believe you."

"So? What's she going to do? Have a fit in front of my relatives?"

Now it's me with the bug-eyes. "You're lying to your mom? I must be a good influence."

Katie laughs as we hurry down the street. "I'm not as big a nerd as you think. I've started doing lots of bad stuff. In choir, half the time I don't even know the words. I just move my mouth and smile." Katie still has a ways to go in the sinning department, but I'm glad to see she's taking a few steps in the right direction.

As we walk, we talk about my problem: do I get rid of the pictures, or keep them in case I need to make the McCreadys back off about my break and enter?

"Well, first of all," she says, "you don't even know for sure if you're in trouble. Why don't you call home and find out?" Katie's pretty smart when she wants to be.

I use the pay phone at the corner. Mom answers. I tell her I'm with Katie and called in case she was wondering where I was. Mom is surprised. She thanks me for being considerate and says to hurry home because supper is about ready. I can tell she thinks I'm up to something.

Before she has a chance to ask me anything, I say, "Any messages?"

"Yes. Jason called. Something about missing you in the parking lot. But he said not to worry, he'll see you tomorrow about what you were looking for. What were you looking for?"

"Nothing. I'll be home right away. Bye." Click.

I'm having a hemorrhage, but Katie gets me to calm down. Obviously Jason knows I was there and stole the Polaroids. Equally obviously, he hasn't done anything about it. And he's not going to, she says.

"But what about this 'see me tomorrow' bit? What's that supposed to mean?"

"He's trying to scare you. Come on, what can he say? 'Leslie stole my pictures of a bunch of naked underage girls?' I'll bet he's peeing himself wondering what *you're* going to do. Like, did you ever stop to think maybe he called to find out if you'd told?"

I'm amazed. Who would have thought that Katie could be sneaky? Either I've been a *really* good influence, or reading all those Nancy Drew books paid off. Anyway, according to her, I don't even need the pictures, as long as Jason thinks I have them. "Your only problem is if they get found. If I were you, I'd ditch them. That way Jason's history, and you're home free. Before you know it, life will go back to normal, and you can pretend none of this ever happened."

This makes sense, except for the last part. I'm good at pretending, but not that good.

Together we take a vow of silence. I even let Katie say a prayer. Then I pull out my Bic and set the photos on fire, one by one. I watch as they burn away. The final stub-ends I toss down a drain hole.

All of a sudden, the pressure's gone. It's up in smoke. I can breathe again. I'm free.

I wish I knew who the other girls were. I wish I could tell them they're free too.

Twenty-six

The next morning, I wake up thinking about Jason's message. I know Katie says to relax, but I can't. No way I want to see Jason until he has time to cool down.

So I start coughing in my room loud enough for Mom to hear. "I don't feel well."

Mom comes in and touches my forehead. "You're fine."

"I'm not." Cough, cough.

Mom sighs, brings me the thermometer and goes to make breakfast. I rub it till it reads a couple of degrees high. Then I join her. "See?"

She knows I'm faking. She shakes it down and makes me do it again, this time watching me like a hawk.

"Do you mind?" I garble, lolling the thermometer around in my mouth. "I can do this myself, you know."

"I'm not stupid, and you're not skipping."

"I'm not skipping, I'm sick."

We fight all through breakfast. I make sure to cough so much my throat hurts for real. As for Mom, she gets a headache. "Leslie, I don't have time to argue any more. Get dressed. You're going to be late."

"You want me to infect the whole school? Talk about considerate. I hope it's meningitis. I hope I die, so you can feel guilty. And I hope you get it too. That'll be a laugh, watching you hack away with double pneumonia."

She puts on her coat. "I'm not writing a note."

"Great. Get me expelled, why don't you?"

She leaves.

If you're going to skip, it's better to do it with a friend. Being stuck all alone gets tired real quick. I flick around the TV. Nothing but news, cartoons and the Shopping Network. I watch a little Teletubbies. I wish I was stoned.

Then the phone rings. I answer with my sick voice. It's the school attendance secretary, calling because I've been marked absent first period.

"I'm sick. My mom'll write a note."

"And what about yesterday? You left without signing out."

"I was too busy puking, do you mind? What are you? The CIA?" I hang up.

I turn off the TV. I walk around the apartment a couple of dozen times. I make faces in the mirror. I'm so bored I even read the newspaper. The headlines, anyway. When I get this bored at Dad's, I sometimes watch the porno tape he keeps at the back of his filing cabinet under his old tax returns. *Behind the Green Door.* I think it was a present from his stag party back when he married Mom. The hairstyles kill me, and the guys all have zits on their bums. I used to find it funny, but since all this stuff started happening with Jason, even the thought of it makes me feel like heaving.

The phone rings again. I figure it's the secretary calling back. Or Mr. Carrouthers. I answer with my sick voice. "I told you, I'm sick."

But it's not the school.

"You can't fool *me,* angel." Jason's voice is very even. "You took something of mine."

Heartbeat. "Correction. *You* took something of *mine.*"

He laughs. Stops laughing. "I want those pictures back."

"I don't think so."

Pause. "Is your mother home?"

"What's it to you?"

A long pause. "I know where you live." Click.

Now I really do feel sick. I let myself down onto the couch and try to breathe. Does that mean he's coming over? Now? Sometime?

How can I keep him out? Our building doesn't have a security guard. The outside door downstairs is locked, but he could get in whenever a tenant comes or goes. I know. I've let in lots of strangers and seen others do it too. If they look respectable, you don't mind. If they don't, you don't want to get them mad.

The phone rings. I think it's him. It rings again. What if it's the school? Rings again. I'll say I was sleeping and didn't hear it. Rings again. And again and again and again, until I can't stand it any more. I pick it up.

Silence on the other end of the line.

"Who is it?"

Breathing.

"I said, 'Who is it?'"

Breathing.

If only Mom wasn't cheap, we'd have call display. I slam the receiver down and dial *69 to find the last number that phoned here. I don't recognize it. I call anyway. It rings and rings and rings. Then someone picks up.

"Is that you, Jason?" I say, trying to keep my voice from shaking.

Silence.

"Listen, asshole, I'm calling the operator. You're in big trouble."

I hang up. I report the number. But there's nothing the operator can do. The call came from a laundromat.

This place is too creepy. I have to get out, go for a donut or something. I have a shower. Get dressed.

Just as I'm doing up my coat, there's a knock on the door. Help. I don't make a sound. Another knock. It's probably not him—but what if? "Who is it?" Silence. I tiptoe to the door. I check through the peephole. I can't see anyone. I keep the chain on and open it a crack. The elevator door down the hall is closing. The corridor's empty.

That's strange.

I take the chain off and open the door wide, ready to head out. And there at my feet is an envelope. My palms start to sweat. I open it. It's a Get Well card. There's a personal note inside.

In sickness and in health,

Yours forever,

Love,

J.

I lock the door and stay inside for the rest of the day.

Twenty-seven

That night, Mom and I keep our distance. She doesn't ask if I went to school, and I don't tell her I didn't. I'm going to school tomorrow, though. I have to face him sooner or later, so I might as well do it with other people around for protection. And besides, hiding out breaks my Number One Rule for trouble at school or at home: Never let them see you're scared.

I get to school minutes before the bell rings. Katie, Ashley and the others are talking at the lockers. Katie gives me a smile and a finger-wave. She's about to say something when suddenly her eyes go wide, like they do when she's watching horror movies. I turn. It's Jason.

"What do you want?"

"Don't I even get a hello?"

"As in, go to Hell-o?" I say it loud, so everyone will be watching in case he tries to yank me away.

But he doesn't. He shakes his head, sad and soulful. "There you go again. That's exactly why I broke up with you."

For the first time in my life, I'm speechless.

"Your attitude. Your temper," he goes on. "Not to mention the other stuff."

"What are you talking about?"

"Do I have to say it in public?" He pretends to whisper, but it's loud enough for everyone to hear. "Last Saturday? That guy feeling you up at the rave?"

"You are such a liar."

"Whatever you say. I don't care any more. I've had it." Jason glances around at the eavesdroppers. "Sorry. I didn't mean to make a scene." They look away, embarrassed. Except for Ashley. He flashes the baby blues and winks at her. "Hi." Then the jerk swivels and saunters off down the hall.

Ashley acts casual, but I know what she's feeling.

"Don't," I warn her.

"Don't what?" she smiles, all innocence.

"Just don't."

"You're not my mother."

"He's not what you think."

"How do you know what I think?"

"Trust me."

"As if." And she struts off to class with her nose so high I picture it scraping the ceiling.

Katie takes my arm. "Even if we told, she'd never believe us," she says in my ear. "Besides, it's not like he asked her out or anything."

That's true. Let's hope it stays that way. I don't want anything on my conscience.

By the end of school, I've relaxed. I even figure Jason doing a little flirting with Ashley is kind of good news, because it means he's not taking the breakup so hard after all. Who cares if he pretends it was me who got dumped? He's off my case. That's what I'm thinking on my way home from school, anyway. The idea makes me so happy I turn my Walkman way up and sing along.

I'm so in this other world I almost run right into him. He's ridden up on his motorcycle and blocked the sidewalk. I pull off my earphones. "What do you want?"

"We have things to talk about."

A heartbeat, then loud and firm: "You're not getting them back. And if you don't leave me alone—RIGHT NOW—I'm taking them to the police."

"Sure you are," he mocks. "You don't want people seeing those pictures any more than I do."

I toss my head. "I wouldn't count on that."

"I admire your guts, breaking into my room like that. It's given me a new respect for you."

"Save it for someone who gives a shit." I start to move around him.

"Hey, come on, don't be such a tease."

I'm past him.

"Where're you going?"

I don't answer. I don't look back. I move fast. He revs his engine. He starts following me, slow, motor almost idling. He could run me down if he wanted. "You're not supposed to be on the sidewalk," I say, hard.

He laughs, guns his motorcycle onto the road, races to the end of the block and wheels around to face me. I turn and start walking back the way I came. I hear him gun the engine. He rides past me, turns back up onto the sidewalk and faces me again. "Fancy meeting you here."

"Get lost, Jason."

"That's my girl," he winks. "Make me hot."

I spit at him, but nothing comes out. My mouth's too dry.

"I wouldn't do that again."

"Oh, really? You want to beat me up on a public street? Go ahead. There'll be witnesses. I wouldn't be surprised if someone's watching out their window right now."

"There won't *always* be witnesses."

"What's that supposed to mean?"

His eyes go dead, like before he'd do it to me. "I love you, Leslie," he says. And with that, he revs his engine. Before I can think to scream, the motorcycle lurches towards me. At the last second, it swerves back to the road and he takes off.

I phone Katie and tell her, the minute I get home. I can hear her swallow. "He's probably playing games. Pretty soon he'll get bored and move on."

"Or do something."

"Don't talk like that. It scares me."

"You've never seen that look of his. So far, okay, maybe it's all been a game. But what happens when he figures he's lost? Jason doesn't lose. Ever."

"You're psyching yourself out. He may be a bully, but it's not like he's killed people or anything."

"Yet."

Actually, "yet" is what I want to say, but I don't have the nerve. So instead, I bite my tongue and mumble, "Yeah, you're right."

There's a silence. Then Katie says, "You're not alone, you know."

"I know."

"Love you."

"Me too."

Twenty-eight

Nothing much else has happened for the past week. It hasn't had to. The idea that it might is just as bad. And I can't stop thinking about the possibilities because wherever I turn, it seems like Jason's there.

He's smart about it. He doesn't get too close. But he's always around just the same. In the corridors. Outside my classrooms. At the door to the gym. A couple of tables away in the library. By the pop machines across the cafeteria. Always with that smirky smile and that cool slouch. Sometimes his shades are on, so I can't tell for sure if he's looking at me. But he is.

Luckily, I have Katie. She's dropped everything, including Ashley, to be with me after school. (Mrs. Kincaid would have a fit if she knew.) We put in time until I know Mom'll be back from work, and then Katie walks me home.

For waiting, we mostly go to this little park near the school. It's getting cold, but we huddle up on a bench and watch the world go by. People walking dogs. Kids rollerblading. Moms, some my age, pushing baby carriages. And every so often, a bunch of geriatrics with walkers. They come on outings from the local old folks' home. By the time they all get off the bus, it's time to get back on.

These days I'm a real downer. I don't know how Katie puts up with me. I'm so insane. Like, I hate Jason, but sometimes I find myself missing him, too. Every so often I tuck my head in, squeeze myself into a ball and sob. Katie puts her arm around me and pats my shoulder until I stop. Maybe Beachball was right. Maybe I *should* go on drugs, tranquilizers or something.

Katie tries to cheer me up. "Being happy isn't easy. You have to work at it." Talk about cornball. But Katie looks so serious I can't help smiling. "See. A smile. Good. Now how about a laugh? 'Laugh and the world laughs with you.' That's what Mom says."

"Your mom is mental."

"Come on, Leslie. Remember when you first came here, how you hated leaving Seattle and how miserable you were?"

"Earth to Katie: I'm still miserable."

"Yeah, but you're not crying about being homesick any more."

"Only because I have better things to cry about."

"You know what I mean."

"Yeah, I know what you mean. But Katie, maybe I don't feel like being happy right now. Okay?"

"Okay."

And we sit there, shivering, until it's time to go home.

I haven't told Mom about the breakup, but she knows. I can tell because she's extra nice all of a sudden. Like, even though I haven't been eating much, she hasn't made a big deal about it or given me a lecture about anorexia. She hasn't asked me to clear the table, either. Best of all, she hasn't asked questions.

Last night was a close call, though. She's scraping plates before doing the dishes when out of nowhere she stops, wipes her hands and comes over.

I'm still at the table staring into space, twisting a serviette. Mom puts her hands on my shoulders. I don't look up. "What?"

"You know, honey," she says in her sympathetic mother voice, "somehow things have a habit of working out for the best." That's one of the biggest lies in the world, but part of me likes her saying it, because it means she cares. The other part of me gets mad, because even though the breakup makes me feel terrible, I know it makes her feel great.

I guess I should be grateful. She could have said "I know how you're feeling" or "Don't say I didn't warn you."

I shrug off her hands and get up. "Want some help with the dishes? I can dry."

"That'd be nice," Mom says, totally stunned. "Thanks."

If she wasn't my mother, I might even like her.

This morning when I get to school, everything's normal except for one thing—Jason's nowhere in sight. By noon, I'm starting to have a good time. Maybe I *am* being paranoid. Maybe I *don't* need a bodyguard after school.

It's time for lunch, so I go to my locker to put my books away. I open it. Something falls out. I pick it up.

It's a Polaroid of me and Katie sitting in the park.

Twenty-nine

I show Katie. She goes white as a sheet.

"You still think I'm paranoid?"

Katie tries to control her breathing. "Mom says if you ignore teasing it'll go away."

"That's what every adult says, and it's a lie. Do nothing, and things get worse."

"I know," she says in a scared voice. "But what choice do you have? You can't stop him going where he wants. You can't stop him taking pictures."

She's right. I decide to pretend everything's fine, hold my breath and hope for once her mother is right.

I never see Jason. It's almost as if he's disappeared. But at least twice a day when I open my locker, out falls another picture—me coming out of a corner store or going into my apartment building. Sometimes, instead of a picture, there's a card with a cheesy message like "You Complete Me." By the middle of the week, I'm shaking so bad when I get to my locker that it takes forever to land the combination for my lock.

At home, the phone never stops ringing. I let Mom do all the answering. When it's him, there's just a click. Like me, she dials *69. A recording says the number is unavailable. The calls must be coming from a pay phone.

By the end of the week, we start turning off the ringer at

night. I mean, he's even called at two and three a.m. The first couple of times, Mom hurried to answer, thinking it was some emergency. I finally tell her it's Jason.

"You don't know that for sure," she reassures me, stirring her coffee. That's what she *says,* anyway. I guess she doesn't know what to do either.

By Friday, it's all too much. I open my locker before school, out drops another card, and I sink to the floor a nervous wreck. Suddenly, like magic, there he is, lounging against the wall opposite, grinning at me.

"Go away!"

He gives this innocent shrug. "What did I do?"

I'm too freaked out to say anything. But not Katie. She walks right up to him and sticks out her chin. "You know, if you really cared about Leslie, you'd leave her alone!"

"Me leave *her* alone? *She's* the one who won't let go. Calling my place all the time, sobbing to my mother." A glance at me. "I wish you'd stop it, Leslie. It's getting tired." He sounds so sincere, I can't believe it.

"You put cards in my locker," I whimper.

"What cards?" he laughs. "Are you sending yourself cards now? No wonder people think you're a nutbar." He cocks his head at Ashley. "Actually, *you're* the reason I dropped by," he says to her. "I'll catch you later, when Miss Kentucky Fried here has had her meds." He does his famous finger-point, grins and heads off.

Ashley pulls out her books really fast.

"You're not going after him, are you?" Katie asks, alarmed.

"Don't be such a baby-suck," Ashley snaps and hurries off. "Baby-suck." This from someone whose mom won't let her wear eye shadow.

Thirty

I don't eat lunch. I sit with Katie, then go to math. I'm actually looking forward to it, because math puts me to sleep, and sleep is what I need. I usually leave mid-class to snooze in the can, but today I'm too tired. I plan to put my head down on the desk instead.

As always, Mr. Kogawa does his impersonation of a human being, droning away, solving problems on the board and wiping the chalk off with the sleeve of his jacket. But even though half the class is nodding off, I'm so wired it's like I'm on Jolt. All I can think about is Jason. I need some privacy. I put up my hand, Mr. Kogawa waves me off, and in a couple of minutes I'm in the far cubicle of the girls' second-floor washroom. I figure I'll stay till school's over.

After I've read the graffiti for the millionth time, I start to nod off—until, out of nowhere, I feel the hairs on the back of my neck stand up. It's the weirdest thing. Like when I pick up the phone to call Katie and she's already on the line. Or when I'm in a place for the first time but it's like

I've been there before. Or when I suddenly know I'm being stared at. Like now.

I lean over and check the floor on all sides outside the cubicle. No feet. Of course not. The can was empty when I got here, and no one's come in since. I'm just freaking myself out. I sit back down, take a few deep breaths. Then this long, slow horror fills me. What if the stare is coming from above?

I look up, afraid of what I'll see. Sure enough, there he is. Jason. He's standing on the toilet lid in the cubicle next to me, staring down.

I want to run for it. But if I do, he could hop out and grab me. So I sit there, frozen, like a mouse in front of a snake.

"You're late," he whispers.

"What...?" I struggle to breathe.

"You're usually here by one-thirty."

"You've been hiding there all along?"

He smirks. I feel sick.

"It's your own fault," he says. "How else am I supposed to talk to you? You hang up the phone. You don't even say thanks for the cards."

"I thought you wanted Ashley."

"Got you jealous, didn't I?"

I'm about to say, "In your wet dreams, pencil dick," but I bite my tongue. "You better get out of here. Someone could catch you."

"So what? If they do, *you'll* be the one in trouble."

"Pardon?"

"I'll say you brought me in here for sex."

My lip quivers.

"Come on, Leslie, don't be like that. I only wanted to teach you a lesson. I miss you. I need you." And now he starts talking like a Hallmark card, like he used to do after he hit me. How his life was nothing before he met me and I'm his "special someone" and he's so sorry and blah blah blah. "I mean it, Leslie," he pleads, "without you I'll die."

"Good!"

"Good?"

"Yeah. Go ahead and die." Saying it feels great. So great I don't even think about the consequences. I keep going, getting braver with every word. "What use are you, anyway? You just waste space. So go ahead. Jump off a building. Swallow a medicine cabinet. You think I care?"

Jason's face contorts. For an instant, I think he's going to cry. Then—WHAM WHAM WHAM—he smashes the wall of the cubicle with his fist. I squinch my eyes and raise my hands as if his fist could break right through.

He crashes out of his cubicle. He stands in front of my door. He gives it a boot. It shakes on its moorings. He boots it again. And again.

Just when I think it's going to break off its hinges, he stops. "You'll be sorry," he whispers through the crack. Then he turns on his heel, like nothing's happened, and walks out whistling.

Thirty-one

All of a sudden, the pictures and phone calls have stopped. But not the cards. They keep getting slipped through my locker door. Just three, but that's enough.

Katie says the fact there're only three is a sign he's getting bored; a few more weeks and he'll leave me alone for good. I wish I believed her, but I don't. These cards are different. Instead of being full of sucky love crap, they're the kind you get after a death in the family—"In Memoriam," "Deepest Sympathy," "With the Angels."

"Leslie, if you really think they're death threats—*tell!*"

"Tell what? There's no handwriting. Nothing to prove they're from him. If I say anything he'll deny it and I'll get accused of being sick, of trying to get attention, of acting out."

Then, last Monday, I opened my locker and there was a dead mouse on top of my books. I screamed. Some other girls screamed too; a few guys laughed.

Later, Katie tried to reassure me. "I doubt if it's from Jason. You're lucky you haven't had mice before, with all those old sandwiches squashed under your gym bag. Besides, he doesn't have your combination, does he?"

"I don't think so."

But I change my lock all the same.

Meanwhile my marks have been going down the toilet. I can't concentrate to study, and as for doing homework, please. Apart from math, which I can do in my sleep, my only decent mark is English.

Katie's marks are down too. Her mom says it's my bad influence and it's got to stop, especially now that exams are coming. That means Katie and I can't spend time together after school; she has to study.

At least she still walks me home, right up to my apartment. And she waits till I've checked the closets and under the beds, too. She says if Jason comes by and starts pounding on the door before Mom gets back from work to call her right away. As if Katie could do anything over the phone.

The worst part of being home alone is having time to think. I think about horrible stuff. Like how last winter there was this boy out west who got stabbed to death and dumped in the bushes. It took months before they found his body; and when they did, it turned out practically all the kids from the local high school knew he was there, they just hadn't told anyone. The adults on TV acted shocked about how the kids could have kept this awful secret. Adults can be pretty stupid.

If I get murdered, I hope Mom won't be mad at me. It's not as if meeting Jason was my fault, exactly. I don't know what it was. Bad luck? Fate? Or maybe God answers prayers after all, to teach people a lesson. I don't know. It doesn't matter. Nothing does.

Katie says it's sick to talk about this, but if Jason kills me, I want to be cremated. I can't stand the idea of being stuck in a box forever. It makes me claustrophobic. I'd like my ashes to be kept in the stone jar we got from Granny P. on her last visit before she died. Mom could keep it on the kitchen counter by the window, next to the African violets. Or, if seeing me there all the time would make Mom sad, I guess she could store them in a closet. Whatever. I just don't want to get buried or scattered.

If you ever read this journal, Mom, I hope you can forget all the awful things I said to you. I didn't mean them. I'm sorry I was a disappointment.

Thirty-two

In scary movies, when a babysitter's alone and hears a strange noise coming from the attic, she always checks it out—even when she knows there's a psycho prowling the neighborhood who goes after babysitters in attics. If Katie and I are watching the movie together, I always elbow her as the babysitter climbs the creaky stairs and her flashlight goes out. "Here comes the chainsaw."

"Tell me when I can look," she squeals, peeking through her fingers.

Part of me thinks those babysitters deserve to die for being so stupid. But the other part of me knows why they do it. It's because the door at the top of the stairs is alive with this overwhelming question: What's on the other side? That question eats in their brains until they're zombies, pulled to their death despite themselves.

I'm in my room cramming for Friday's geography exam when the phone rings. Nothing bad's happened for two days, and I'm getting calm enough to memorize all about semi-arid continental climates.

Mom answers. "Hello? Oh hello, Jason. I'm sorry, but I'm afraid she doesn't want to speak to you."

I perk up. Jason? He identified himself?

"I'll give her the message." Mom sticks her head in. "That was Jason."

I twirl my hair with my pencil and keep staring at my textbook like I couldn't care less. "What did he want?"

"Not much. He called to say goodbye. He says he's been thinking it over, and he's taking your advice."

"Oh," I say absently, but chills run up my spine. My only advice to Jason was to die, just jump off a building or swallow pills. He's taking it? He's called to say goodbye?

"Is he changing schools?" Mom asks.

"I guess so," I yawn.

"Well, that's good. An odd time, though, right before exams."

"An odd time for an odd guy."

Mom laughs. "I'm glad you have your sense of humor back." She gives me the kind of warm mother look that makes me want to hurl. "The first breakup's always tough. But I told you you'd get over it. You know, I remember when I was sixteen—"

"Yeah. Chester Martin. You loved how he hiccupped. You've told me. I'm studying."

"Sorry." And she disappears.

After a quick panic, I reassure myself. No way Jason's going to kill himself. He just wants to wreck my studying. I won't let him.

I try to go back to reading. But I can't. I keep thinking, what if I wake up tomorrow and he really *is* dead? What if those funeral cards weren't about me? What if they were about *him?* What if they were a cry for help? Sure he's a creep and I hate him, but if he dies, how will I ever live with myself?

I decide to call. If he really *is* killing himself, maybe I can talk him down or call an ambulance. But I can't call from here. I don't want to risk Mom listening in on the extension, like I do when she's talking to Dad. There's a pay phone at the end of the street.

"I need a break," I say, grabbing my coat. "I'm going for a walk to the corner store, maybe pick up some gum."

"Oh, could you get milk while you're there?"

"Sure."

She gives me some money.

"Back in a few minutes."

All of a sudden I get this crazy thought. What if Jason can read my mind? Like, what if his call is part of a plan to get me outside now it's dark? What if he's waiting in the bushes? Hardly anyone's on the street at night, and I have to pass a couple of alleyways and—this is nuts. Am I a prisoner in this dump or what?

All the same, just to be safe, I go back to my room and

write a quick note: "If anything happens to me, it's Jason." I put the note on my desk under my geography book. That way Mom won't walk in and find it by accident, but it's there just in case.

Outside, I walk fast, crossing the street whenever I get near an alley. They're all empty, except for one with a kid huffing airplane glue. "You're gonna get zits all around your lips," I shout across the street. He looks up sort of glazed and scared of being caught. "Yeah," I go on, "and then your brains are gonna fall out!" Okay, I've done my bit to save his life, now time to think about saving Jason's.

I get to the pay phone feeling like a total drama queen. I make the call. The phone rings and rings and rings. At first, my chills come back—is Jason somewhere around here watching? But the longer it rings, the more I start to worry. What if it's true and he's already done it? Shot his brains out? Slit his throat? Hung himself? Should I call the police? Call his cottage? Call a cab?

I'm about to hang up and call *somebody*, when at the last minute he picks up. "Hello?" He doesn't sound so good, but maybe he's putting on a sick voice.

"What's your message supposed to mean?"

"Leslie, I'm glad you called. I wanted to hear your voice one last time. My parents are at the cottage. Tonight's the night."

"For what?"

"I've got a quart of Jack Daniels and a bunch of my mother's pills. You'll never have to see me again."

"Come on, Jason. No way you're killing yourself."

"Let's not fight."

"Look, I don't have time for this. I have an exam tomorrow."

"Then go home and study." There's a pause. "I've left some stuff for you on the pool table."

"What stuff?"

"A letter. About how you were right. How I don't deserve to live."

"You left a letter blaming me?"

"It doesn't blame you. It thanks you. You made everything clear."

"That's sick."

"There's also one last Polaroid from our first night. You never found it 'cause it wasn't in the box. I kept it in my wallet. I'll put it with the letter and whoever finds it will pass it on. It's got your name on it."

Oh my God. "No, Jason. Burn it."

"Goodbye, Leslie."

"I said, burn it!"

But it's like he doesn't hear me. "Have a good life. I loved you. I'll always watch over you." Click.

I hear the dial tone. For a second, I freak. Then I'm angry. He's playing mind games. What kind of fool does he take me for?

I go into Happy Grocery breathing fire, pay for the milk and ask for a pack of smokes. The cashier asks for my ID.

"I don't have it with me."

"Then sorry."

"Don't 'sorry' me!" I yell. "You're the only stupid store in the whole world that asks for ID, so get real."

The woman grabs a broom and tells me to get out or she'll call the cops.

"Happy Grocery, my ass," I snarl, and I take off.

I go back to the pay phone, ready to rumble. I call Jason again. It rings I don't know how many times. I picture him laughing to himself as he listens. Then I picture him slipping into a coma from his mother's pills and booze. I go from mad to scared. I think about phoning the suicide prevention line or even the cops, but I can't take the chance. What happens if there really *is* a note and a picture? They'll call me a slut and a murderer.

I start pacing a bit outside the phone booth, talking to myself. It seems to help me think. I remember to whisper and not move my lips, though. I don't want to attract attention, like Marge with the shopping cart outside Katie's church.

"What's the big deal? Just go over," I say.

"What, are you crazy?" I answer back.

"If Jason dies and you don't go, you'll blame yourself as long as you live. Plus, going means you'll get that picture and letter."

"But what if he's bluffing?"

"He won't do anything while he thinks you have the Polaroids. He hasn't touched you since you stole them, has he? And you left that note in your room for insurance."

It's settled. I'm going over. But not alone.

I call Katie.

"Hellew." It's Mrs. Kincaid, using her classy voice.

"Hi, it's Leslie. Can I please speak to Katie?"

"I'm afraid Katie is studying for her exams."

"I know. But this is an emergency."

"It will have to wait till tomorrow."

"But—"

"Goodbye, dear." Click.

I wait a minute and call back, hoping this time it'll be Katie.

"Hellew?"

I hang up. Another few minutes, and I call again.

But Mrs. Kincaid knows this game. "Leslie, am I going to have to speak to your mother?"

I hang up. I guess I'm going by myself after all.

There's a drunk passed out on a nearby park bench. I leave the milk from Happy Grocery next to his booze and grab a passing cab. I can pay with the change from the ten Mom gave me. Lucky I didn't get smokes after all. Was that fate? Or a guardian angel?

Mom'll be wondering where I am. She'll be worried and mad. But I don't have time to think about that. I'm on a mission of life and death.

Thirty-three

The cab pulls up in front of the McCreadys'. There are no cars in the driveway, no lights. I ask the driver to wait, but he's a little suspicious and wants to see some money. I've only got enough for the ride, which leaves me with a quarter. He swears, tells me to get the hell out and takes off.

I go up the walk, ring the doorbell. Nobody comes. I rap the brass knocker. The front door opens by itself. It must have been ajar all along.

There's a bunch of light switches on the wall to the right. I reach in and flick them all on. Then I step inside, leaving the front door wide open.

"Jason?"

Silence.

I take a second to think. The note and the picture are supposedly on the pool table, but they can wait. The first thing I have to do is find Jason. If he's dying, I need to call emergency right away. If he's not, I don't want him coming downstairs after me, trapping me in the basement.

I figure if he's taken pills, he's probably upstairs on his bed. That's where I'd be if I was going to OD. First, to be comfy. Second, to be considerate to my mom. "She looks so peaceful, just like she's sleeping," she'd think. Even if that's not a *great* comfort, it beats getting found with your bum sticking out of a gas oven and the house ready to blow. Or with your brains decorating the wallpaper.

The idea that he may be in a coma makes me want to run up to his bedroom right away. But in case it's a trap, I say in a loud voice, "You stay behind that bush, Katie. If I'm not back in two minutes, call the cops." Then I check the main floor, peeking in obvious hiding spots like the front hall closet and turning on all the lights as I go, even the lamps and the little light over the stove. On top of that, I check the garage and poke my head out the back door. He's nowhere.

Now for his bedroom. "Just another two minutes, Katie," I call out. Then I go to the foot of the staircase, flick on the upstairs hall light and head up.

I hurry to his room at the end of the corridor. Along the way, I glance into the other rooms in case he's inside one of them, waiting to pounce. The rooms are dark. But empty. I turn on their lights and keep moving.

And now I'm at his door. It's shut tight. "Jason?" I throw it open. What a mess. But no Jason.

I get a panic flash that he's back down the hall hiding in his parents' ensuite bathroom. I imagine him blocking my exit and—zoom—I fly down the stairs, three at a time, and race out the front door, gasping for breath.

Home free. I fall on the grass and laugh. I feel a bit hysterical from sheer relief.

But it's not over yet. There's still the basement—the furnace, laundry and rec rooms. And in the rec room, the pool table where he said I'd find the Polaroid and the note.

No problem, I tell myself. There's lights everywhere now. The front door is open. I have a clear, well-lit escape route.

"Okay, Katie, keep me covered." It occurs to me I might be giving the neighbors a show. I look across the street, but the living rooms are all either dark or have their curtains drawn. Right. Around here everyone has families, and family rooms to put them in.

I take a deep breath and go back inside. I get to the basement stairs and start down. But something feels wrong. Like I'm going into a burial vault.

"Turn back," I tell myself.

But my feet won't listen. That Polaroid is so close. A few more steps and I'll have it. Even if this is a set-up, Jason won't do anything as long as he thinks Katie's outside.

So I keep going, like one of those zombie babysitters.

I'm at the rec room door. It's wide open. Inside, everything's dark. I feel for the light switch, half afraid Jason's going to grab my hand.

I find the switch. Click. Light floods the room. Good—he's not here. I start towards the pool table, but there's nothing. No note. No Polaroid. Oh God. It's a trap! I shouldn't have come.

And now, from upstairs, the sound of the front door closing. Footsteps. And somebody coming downstairs.

It's him.

Jason enters the rec room slowly, shutting the door behind him. "Hi." No smile. Nothing.

Don't show him you're scared, I think. "Oh, you're okay. I was worried."

"I'll bet."

"Really," I stammer. "So where's the last Polaroid?"

"There isn't one."

"Oh," I gulp. "Well, if there isn't one, and you're okay, I might as well be going."

He doesn't move from the door. "You're not going anywhere."

We stand there for I don't know how long, squaring off. Then I hear myself say, "Katie's outside. Let me go or she'll call the cops."

"Bullshit. I watched through the curtains. You came by yourself."

My stomach flips up my throat. "Where did you hide? I looked everywhere."

"Behind the furnace. I figured you'd head to the rec room right away, but you're full of surprises." His lip twitches. "When you ran out, I went to see what was up. I was right behind the front door when you came back in."

"Well, ha, ha, ha, aren't you clever." I struggle to act sarcastic. "Is that supposed to make me scared?"

A flicker in his eyes. "You're pretty smart for a dead girl."

"Very funny."

But he isn't laughing.

"Okay," I say, "you win. Now let me go. Remember those other Polaroids. If I get hurt—"

"Those Polaroids are history."

"Says who?"

"Me. You're too chicken to keep them. Not that I care. I mean, who's to say I took them? And if I did, so what?

Photography's my hobby. You wanted to pose. It's just private boyfriend/girlfriend stuff. Anyway, Dad'll fix any problems. He always does." Jason smiles. "Nobody makes a fool of me. Especially not some scaggy ho. Some skank pig slut. Who do you think you are, anyway?"

He starts to move around the pool table. I move too, keeping it between us. "Don't, Jason," I scramble. "Even if Katie's not outside, she knows I'm here."

"Who cares? You may be here, but I'm not. I'm up at the cottage with my folks. Ask them. Wanna bet what they'll say?" Suddenly he leaps over the table, grabs my elbows and runs me back into the wall. He presses against me. "I could kill you now if I wanted," he breathes in my ear.

"You better not. There'll be blood. DNA!"

"Just if you're cut." He licks my neck. "But I can strangle you with your panties. Toss you in the trunk of Mom's car. Dump you in a secluded spot."

The two other girls in the pictures. What did he do to them?

"God, you're sweet." He nuzzles my ear.

I want to knee him, bite into his cheek, but then he'd kill me for sure, so instead I yell.

"Shut up!" He slaps the side of my head. "No one can hear you down here, so just shut up!" His voice is like fists. I crumple to the floor, sobbing.

"Yeah. Cry for me. I like it."

"You're sick!"

His mouth twists. "You have no idea." And now he

backs away, breathing heavy, leans against the pool table. "Reality check, Leslie. You skip school, do drugs, lie, act like a slut. You're a bottom-feeder. Totally disposable. Knowing everyone was gone from my place, you broke in. You stole money, jewelry, then hit the streets. A teen runaway. It happens every day."

I'm hyperventilating. "I left Mom a note. You're blamed if anything happens."

"Oh?" He grins. "You wrote her a lie to get me in trouble?"

"She'll call the cops. They'll come."

"We'll be long gone." He picks up a pool cue.

"They'll know it was you."

"They can know what they like. They'll never prove it." He strokes the pool cue. "Now on your feet. It's time for your lesson."

I get up, blubbering. Stand there while he looks me over.

"Okay, bitch," he says, eyes dead. "Strip."

I fumble my hands to the top button of my jeans. As soon as I take off my clothes, he'll kill me. I don't know how I know it, but I do. I turn away, hunch over, pretend to unbutton. Dear God, let me live and I promise to be perfect from now on.

"Face me," he says.

My right hand slips into my pocket.

"I said, turn around!" he barks. "Gimme a show!" He jabs me in the back with the end of the cue.

I start moving my shoulders up and down, like a stripper doing an act. Up and down, I wiggle towards him, up and down, still faced away.

"Yeah! Toss in some ass!"

Up and down, hand deep in my pocket. Up and down, hand searching. Up and down. I've found what I need.

"Face me, bitch!"

And I do. Fast. Hand out of my pocket. House keys clenched between my knuckles. I slash across his face full force. I rip an eyelid.

"Aaa!!!" He staggers back. "You'll pay for that!"

The tip of the pool cue whizzes by my ear. It slices the air again and again as he swings, blood in his eyes. "You're dead!"

I duck under the pool table as the cue smacks down. It cracks across the side pocket, snaps. I do a side-roll under the table, hop to my feet, run to the door and throw it open.

But he's behind me. Grabs my hair. Yanks me back. I'm on the table.

"You wanna play games?" He raises the broken end of the cue.

My hand's on a billiard ball. I pitch wild. It hits him in the mouth. Stunned, he falls back, howls. Charges again. Stabs the jagged cue end into the table.

"Die, bitch!"

But I've squirmed away. I'm up the stairs. I'm out the front door. I'm screaming all the way up the street.

Thirty-four

Does anyone hear me?

If they do, I doubt they'll even check it out. This is a nice, quiet neighborhood, where everyone minds their own business. That is, until the cops and ambulances show up, along with the TV cameras, and bodies get hauled off to the morgue. Then everyone acts all surprised. "Well, we heard *something,* but we thought it was kids horsing around." Or a cat. Or a car backfiring. Anything except somebody getting raped or shot or beaten to death. 'Cause that only happens other places. Not here.

I see myself on a porch, banging away, him coming, and the people inside bolting the door. "We don't want any trouble. Go away!" Is that what they'd really do? I don't know. But I can't afford to find out. I've got to get away from here *now.*

I check over my shoulder, but Jason hasn't followed. Instead, he's closed his front door and turned off the lights, except for the fancy lantern by the steps. His house looks like every other house on the street. Even if people around here did come to the window, what would they see? Some crazy girl screaming.

Lucky for me, a bus comes up as I hit the shelter. I flash my transit pass at the driver, head to the back seat and slouch down, so if Jason drives by I'll be hidden.

My mind's racing. How bad is his cut? Will it need

stitches? Can he charge me with assault? Wouldn't that be a joke. But typical. So far, I don't even have a bruise. I wish I did. If I looked beat up, maybe somebody'd believe me. Or maybe not. Beachball would probably say I did it to myself. After all, Jason's dad is a Somebody. And she wouldn't be the only one to side with him. Practically the whole world would. After all, it'd be my word against the McCreadys. Guess who'd win.

I get to the subway. The last time I ran from Jason's house, with the Polaroids, I felt safe underground. Not now. I picture him racing down to the platform, pushing me onto the rails. They'd call it an accident. I imagine the crowd watching as I'm hosed off the tracks, pissed that I've delayed their ride.

Now things start to happen like in a dream. I mean, I know where I am and I know what I'm doing, but it's as if I'm somebody else. I'm separate from my body, watching myself do things: getting on the train, going past my stop, transferring to the line that takes me to the commuter station downtown.

Who can I trust? Mom and Katie. Maybe Ms. James. Can they protect me? Don't make me laugh. He wants me dead. He knows where I live. He'll get what he wants.

Unless I go someplace he won't think about. Dad's.

I get off at the commuter station. The first thing I have to do is call home. Mom will be going wild.

I drop my last quarter into the pay phone. She picks up on the first ring. "Leslie?"

"Yeah."

"Where are you? What's happened?"

"Nothing," I say. "Everything's fine."

"*Fine?* You leave for the store—"

"Don't yell at me."

"Leslie, I want you back here right now!"

"I can't. Something's come up."

"Right now!"

"I said, no. I'm not coming back! Ever! Know why? Because you always yell at me!" I hang up and walk around in circles, slapping my legs. Why is she always like this? Then I'm ashamed. I've crapped up her life so bad. It'll be better for her with me gone. She'll see that once she's had time to cool down. It's sort of a silver lining.

I head outside to bum the money to get to Oakville.

These days, there's so much competition in the panhandling department, it's hard to make a buck. An old guy, maybe forty, offers to help me out, wink, wink, but I shout in his face, "Does your wife know you're out screwing kids?" He takes off fast as the space shuttle.

I decide I need a sob story. "I'm a runaway. Please help me go home," I cry to anyone who'll listen. The first part is true, and the second part is sort of true, considering that's what Dad and Brenda call Oakville. It goes to show that people can tell the truth and still be liars. Truth is complicated.

At last I meet this middle-aged woman. She's going a couple of towns farther, but says she'll buy me a ticket if I'll sit with her on the train. I figure this condition is to make sure I'm not lying about wanting the money for a ticket.

Well, that's only half of it. Turns out she's a Jehovah's Witness, so all the way to Oakville I'm listening to her talk about being saved. I want to tell her to take a hike. But me listening is making her day, so I just sit tight and chalk it up as a good deed.

As we pull into Oakville she gives me money for a cab to Dad's and a copy of the *Watchtower*, which she pulls from a small pile in her bag. I say thanks, and how someday I'll drop by the Kingdom Hall and get more information. Then I run.

Thirty-five

I don't know what I expect from Dad. After the Brenda blowout, I'd told him that since he didn't have time for me Saturdays, I didn't have time for him Sundays. I only planned to make that punishment last a few weeks, but by then I was up to my ears in Jason.

Dad took me to lunch a couple of times. I ate fast, then said I had to go get ready for a date. He acted all smarmy, said he was happy I had a boyfriend and he'd leave it to me to let him know when I had time for a visit. By the time Jason and I broke up, I was out of the habit of seeing him.

I've called, but it's usually Brenda who's answered. Lately, Dad hasn't been in. "He's working late."

"Like when he was working late with *you?*" I want to laugh. "Well, boo hoo. What you did to Mom, someone's doing to you." But that's not what I say. Instead, I go super sympathetic. "Gee, Brenda, I'm *verrry, verrry* sorry. You must be *devastated.*" (That's way better—mean but polite, and points for vocab.) Then I hang up and picture her crying, all alone in what should have been Mom's and my apartment.

But this is the problem of doing-unto-others—drop a turd on somebody's plate and tomorrow you'll be eating their leftovers. That's what I'm thinking as I buzz Dad's apartment. Because now I'm the one with the problem and she's the one who gets to turn the screws.

"Who is it?" She's even Cute and Perky over the intercom.

"It's me. Is Dad there?"

"Dave, it's Leslie." Good, he's home for once. BZZZ.

I open the door and go to the elevator. The lobby doesn't smell so new any more. But unlike at our place, the carpets aren't crusty, the windows are clean and there are real plants, not just green plastic dust magnets.

Dad and Brenda are waiting by the elevator door when it opens. He scoops me out and hugs me. "Leslie. Your mother called. You had us worried sick." He's so embarrassing when he tries to act like a father. I want to say, "Chill out." But instead, I hold on and cry. I don't care who sees.

We go to their apartment. Dad gets me settled in the kitchen and asks Brenda to make some hot chocolate while he phones Mom to say I've been found.

"I wasn't lost. And don't call Mom."

He kneels in front of my chair and holds my hands. "Leslie, we have to."

"Why can't I just stay here and nobody know?"

Dad looks at Brenda to see what to say, but for once she's smart and keeps her mouth shut. For once he's smart too. Instead of talking, he asks a question. "Leslie . . . What's going on?"

The air chokes up my nose. "Nothing." An awful silence. He watches me sniffle. "It's just . . . we always fight. She always yells. I don't want to be there. I want to be here with you."

Another awful silence.

"Leslie . . . What's *really* going on?"

"Why? Don't you want me?"

"Of course we do. But right now, we need you to tell us the truth."

"You won't believe me."

"Trust us."

I gulp and give Brenda a look. She gets the message and leaves, giving Dad's shoulder a little rub as she passes. I look into his eyes. My lip trembles. I hear myself say, "A guy wants to kill me."

"What guy?"

In the background, I hear Brenda calling Mom. I don't care any more.

"The guy I was going out with. Jason McCready. He knows where I live."

Dad takes this in. "Leslie," he says carefully, "sometimes people say things they don't mean."

"He's tried!"

"Leslie?" He gives me a questioning look.

"I knew you wouldn't believe me."

"I do." He doesn't. "Why don't we call his parents? Get to the bottom of this." What a dork. I pull my hands away, cross my arms and start to rock.

"We can call the police, too," he adds fast. "Would that make you feel better? Maybe they can drop by, talk to him, straighten this out."

"No! Talking won't help."

Dad closes his eyes for a second, like I'm being difficult. Then he says, all gentle and earnest, "Leslie, what else can we do?"

"Nothing!" I look right at him. "Nothing! That's what I've been trying to tell you! It's why I'm here! It's why you have to protect me!"

"Of course I'll protect you."

"You won't. You'll send me back to Mom!"

"Okay, okay." He clicks his tongue. "For tonight, how about you sleep here in your room?" My room—that's what he calls the spare room when I'm around. "You get a good night's sleep and tomorrow we'll see what we can do."

Brenda shows up in the doorway. "I talked to Linda. She'll be here in half an hour," she says to Dad in this stage whisper, like maybe I'm deaf or something.

My eyes go wide.

"I'll call her right back," Dad reassures me, squeezing my hand. "Don't you worry. You're staying here."

"Dave?"

He shoots Brenda a glance. "Just deal with the hot chocolate, will you?" He picks up the phone on the wall by the fridge and punches in the number. "Linda, it's Dave." He must have got her just before she left.

Listening to one side of their conversation is hard. I keep wanting to add things, important things, but he keeps waving me down like he can handle it. Which he can't.

"Apparently, there's this boy . . . Jason, right . . . He's made a threat. She's scared sick . . . I told her that . . . Yes, I told her that . . . Yes, I told her that too . . . All right then. We'll see you in half an hour." He hangs up.

"You said I could stay here."

"You can. Your mother's just coming out. We all need to talk."

"She'll make me go back. She will. You'll let her."

"I won't."

"You will! And he'll kill me!"

"Leslie—"

"Liar! Coward!" And I bolt from the room and out the door.

Dad chases me down the hall. "Come back!"

Forget the elevator; stairs are faster. I fly like a bat out of hell. I hit the lobby, and I'm gone.

Thirty-six

It's cold this time of year, and I don't know where to go. I think of a bus shelter, to at least get out of the wind, but that's way obvious. For sure Mom and Dad'll be driving around looking for me, with Brenda stuck "holding the fort." They'll have cops out after me, too. In the city, big deal. There's lots of street kids, and hostels where I could give a fake name. But in places like this, the nomads stand out.

I end up hiding behind these evergreen bushes along the side of a school a couple of blocks away. They won't think to look for me here—it's too close. As a bonus, there's some heat coming from the building, and I can see the lights in Dad's highrise apartment.

I don't really sleep. My ears are so cold I think they're going to fall off, but when I pull my jacket up over my head my bum freezes. Around two in the morning, I think I see Mom's car drive by. But maybe it isn't her. Then around four I see the lights in Dad's apartment go out. I wonder if she's in the spare room.

By seven, it's getting light. I could hang around here and pretend to be a student, but not even browners get to school this early. If I don't head out soon I'll be spotted by a janitor come to turn on the boiler.

I crawl out from under the bushes. I'm stiff, I'm hungry, and my nose is running. I try hopping up and down to warm up. Some people think kids run away because it's cool, like we're all monkey-see-monkey-do. Right, we really want to get sick and dirty and starve to death because we saw somebody do it on TV.

A car pulls into the parking lot. A janitor. I take off.

I walk around for maybe an hour. There starts to be traffic, people driving to work in the city. I wonder what Jason's doing, if he's back home waiting outside my apartment. And then I see this donut shop.

I go inside. At first I'm self-conscious, what with all the suits there to pick up a coffee and muffin. But then I relax, on account of the grungies. There's this table of guys with hat hair who look as if they're sobering up from an all-nighter. And a woman with so much makeup she's either a hooker or a beautician. And next to the door, this guy with shakes and tattoos who's tapping his feet like he's waiting for his dealer—and his dealer's really really late. Around these guys, I don't smell at all.

I take a seat, rub my hands together and think. What's next? *Really* next. What do I do for food? For money? Last night at the train station was a real wakeup. Whenever I begged before, it was for fun, to see if I could do it, and I had way better luck. Usually enough for a movie inside a half hour. It's weird, but wanting something so bad it hurts makes it harder to get.

Right now I need to eat. I think maybe as soon as I'm warm I'll set up shop outside the front door and guilt the suits leaving for work. Then, in the afternoon, I can find a strip mall, beg outside an electronics store. That way I can watch the TVs through the window if I'm bored.

Someone's staring at me.

I look up in panic and see what passes for the manager—this twenty-something guy in a red-and-white striped shirt and a clip-on bow tie. His hair is all slicked back and he has a big Adam's apple. He points to a sign with block letters and announces in this official voice, "Tables for customers only."

"Thanks a lot," I go, all sarcastic, "but I can read, *Dale.*"

He looks surprised, like he's thinking, "How does she know my name?"

I point at his name tag: "Hi, My Name Is Dale."

"I'm going to have to ask you to leave."

I pull out my wallet. "As a matter of fact, I'm here to order two dozen donuts for my dad. So you better apologize or he'll drop by later and talk to your boss."

Dale's face goes blotchy. "Sorry."

I give him a smirk and join the lineup. I'm glad it's long. I don't have any money and this way I have a while longer to warm up. Also to breathe in the cigarettes. There's so much smoke in here it's like puffing a pack.

"How may I help you?" I look up. It's "Hi, My Name Is Shirley."

I'm at the front of the line. How did that happen? I hear myself say, "I'll have six honey glazed, six walnut crullers, six chocolate glazed and six blueberry jelly, please."

All of a sudden, there's a box with two dozen donuts in

front of me. I think about saying, "These donuts are stale!"
and taking off. But they look so good and I'm so hungry I
just grab the box and run.

Next thing I know, Shirley's yelling, suits are blocking
the door, I'm being held by drunks and Dale's on the
phone to the cops.

Thirty-seven

Officer Maloney is fat with a notepad. He looks like the
kind of guy who gets drunk and makes toasts at dinner
parties. Officer Brant is his partner. She'd be okay if it
weren't for the coffee breath. They're standing on either
side of me out by the cruiser.

I'm too scared to look at their faces. Instead, I look at the
windows of the donut shop. It seems we're quite the topic
of conversation, everyone nodding at each other and pointing. As for Dale, he's strutting around like he'll be getting a
medal from Crimestoppers or something.

Officer Brant does the talking. "Could you show us some
ID?" She looks like a kickboxer.

"Don't have any." I shove my hands into my pockets and
move from side to side. It's so cold.

"Do you have a name?"

"Uh, Melissa Johnson," I say.

"Well, 'Uh, Melissa Johnson,' could you give us your *real*

name?" Officer Brant doesn't crack a smile, but I know she thinks she's funny. So does Officer Maloney.

"My name's Melissa Johnson," I repeat, more confident this time.

"Where do you live?"

"162 Cranberry Street."

"Never heard of it."

"Well, that's where I live." I feel the cold come up through my sneakers.

Officer Brant gets in my face. The reek of Maxwell House makes me gag. "It looks to me like you're underage."

"No way. I'm eighteen."

"When were you born?"

I get the year wrong. And I'm supposed to be good at math.

Now it's Officer Maloney's turn. "Look, 'Melissa,' either you tell us the truth or we arrest you and take you downtown to be fingerprinted."

"For two dozen donuts?"

Maloney flips his notepad shut and goes to the car radio. Officer Brant just stands there, arms folded, and watches me cry.

"Please. They got them back. What more do you want? Just let me go."

Of course they don't. There's a Missing Persons bulletin matching my description. Talk about putting a move on. I heard somewhere cops normally wait a day after a person goes missing in case they're just sulking or something. It doesn't take much to figure Mom or Dad must have mentioned Jason and the threat stuff.

They drive me to the station and put me in this room to wait for my parents. They also bring me some chicken noodle soup. It comes in a paper cup out of a machine, so it's pretty gross, but I don't care. Right now it tastes good.

Officers Maloney and Brant sit around and keep me company. Once they found out they'd got a missing person, they started acting different. I guess that means I'm not going to jail. I don't feel like chatting, though. I just want to have my soup and be by myself. "You don't need to babysit me," I say.

But they don't take the hint. Instead, they make small talk. I guess they figure this is a chance to stay inside and get warm. I decide to tune out. I pretend I'm in physics. We wait forever for Mom and Dad, but when they walk in it feels like no time's passed at all.

I was afraid they'd be mad. But they aren't. They're serious. So serious nobody'd know they actually hate each other's guts.

Somebody else is with them. This woman in a navy dress suit. Maloney and Brant get up.

Mom doesn't wait for introductions. She comes over and hugs me. Then she and Dad shake hands with Maloney and Brant, and I get introduced to the new person, Detective Constable Kissoon. She tells me to call her Sylvia. I don't really look at her, not to be rude or anything, but because I'm nervous.

"Thanks, I'll take it from here," Sylvia says to Maloney and Brant. She asks my parents to wait while she talks to me privately in the room next door. I follow her over. We sit opposite each other with a table between us. Time goes slow again, so slow it's almost in reverse. Sylvia puts a pocket tape recorder on the table and turns it on.

"Try and ignore this," she says.

Right. My palms are sweating. So are my feet. There's no air. I can't breathe. Sylvia catches my eye and holds it. She's smiling, friendly, but firm and controlled, like my old swimming instructor the first time I did the dog paddle across the pool.

Once I'm settled, she asks a few questions. Ordinary questions about how I am and can she get me anything, stuff like that, but I know where things are headed. I mean, she's not paid to be nice. This is to loosen me up so I'll let something slip when the hard questions start.

I know all this, but even so, when the real questions come, I just answer. What's the point of hiding now? If she doesn't want to believe me, fine. At least it's out.

But it's *not* like she doesn't believe me. She keeps nodding, concentrating so hard it's like she's pulling the words out of me with her eyes.

Suddenly, I get scared. I say, "It's not like it's Mom's fault or anything. You're not going to give my dad custody or anything, are you?"

Sylvia shakes her head reassuringly. "No, of course not." Then she smiles again and asks another question. I wonder if she's married. Or has kids. I wonder if she has problems with them, like Mom with me. And now I see she's staring at me waiting for an answer. "Pardon?"

I talk and talk and talk. I talk about earlier, when me and Jason met and how the hitting started. And then she asks about Jason and sex.

"I don't want to talk about it."

Sylvia keeps eye contact and waits.

"Look, it's all in my journal. If you really want to know, just read that."

And at the mention of my journal, the world goes on full alert.

Thirty-eight

It seems my journal is "evidence." If charges are laid against Jason, it'll be important in court.

Evidence. Court. Do I want to go through with it? Sylvia says the police will decide whether or not to lay charges, but they likely won't unless I cooperate. She says if we go ahead, things will be hard. Jason's lawyer will ask tough questions to make me look like a liar. Even if the court believes me, Jason will probably just get a few months in juvenile detention on account of he's only seventeen and hasn't been in trouble before. After that he'll be free.

In one way, laying charges looks pointless. But if I don't,

he'll get away with it. And he can keep coming after me with nobody doing anything until I'm dead.

What drives me crazy is that Jason would officially be considered a first-time offender. Sylvia and I talk about the other girls in the Polaroids. She shows me files of missing kids, but I don't recognize them. And without those girls, there would be no so-called "similar fact evidence" for the judge to consider in sentencing.

Sylvia says I don't have to decide what to do right away; I can take my time, talk to my parents over the next week or two. Meantime, she hooks Mom and me up with something called Victim Services. We'll get deadbolts for our apartment, and I'll get a free cell phone for in case I'm outside and in trouble.

I also get to "see someone." Her name is Dr. Seymour. Apparently she deals with "cases like mine." She's even written a book. That makes me think she must be smarter than that goof we went to for family counseling.

On the school front, Beachball turns out to be unsinkable. The cops asked her what she knew and when she knew it. But guess what? According to her, she had no idea there was a problem. Why, yes, she'd read my journal, and spoken to me immediately, but I told her it was all make-believe. Cover your ass, Ms. Barker, it's big enough.

Beachball says that my missed exams won't count against me. My term work's good enough that I'll either scrape through or get failures bumped to a fifty. But that hardly makes up for the fact that Jason gets to stay in school, and Beachball won't do anything about it. She says if I'd feel more comfortable somewhere else, she'd be happy to arrange a transfer. I'm the one who's been screwed over, and he's the one who gets to stay?

Typical.

Thirty-nine

This morning Mom let me sleep in. Since I'm not back at school yet, I guess she figured there's no point in torturing me. As usual, I stayed inside, deadbolt secured. I'm still too nervous to go out unless I'm with somebody. I'm probably being paranoid. I have my cell phone now and I can't believe Jason would be crazy enough to come after me while the heat's on. But crazier things have happened.

Anyway, I'm sitting in front of the *Teletubbies* having breakfast—a Coke and a slice of cold pizza from last night—when the phone rings. In case it's *him,* I check the call display machine from Victim Services before I pick up. But it's not. It's Sylvia. I grab it.

"I've got something for you to take a look at," she says. "When would be convenient for me to come over?"

"Let me check my date book," I say, thinking I'm being majorly funny. There's a pause while she waits, like she actually thinks I have one. When I realize she's not going to laugh, I say, "Actually, now would be fine."

Sylvia comes right over. I make her an instant coffee. We

sit at the kitchen table like we're two moms at a coffee klatch. Then, once we're settled, she takes a surprise out of her briefcase.

At first I don't get it. Then it clicks. Sylvia may not have a sense of humor, but she sure is smart. I'm staring at a copy of last year's yearbook from Port Burdock Central High. Port Burdock—Jason's old stomping grounds. He was at the private boys' school, but there'd be girls in town.

I flip through. Bang. My eyes are like a magnet. Jill Bentham, 9C. Melanie Brady, 10B. They smile out at me from their class pictures. Is it just me, or is there something in their eyes? Secrets.

Strange. I thought I was done with crying.

I'm hyper all day till four o'clock, when Katie gets here. We sit in the bathroom giving each other facials. Katie thought this would be good for calming me down, seeing as it's a big sin to move your lips while the mask is drying.

I don't care. I talk like a bad ventriloquist. "I caaan't jussst sssit heeere waiiiting. I'vve gooot tooo caaall theeem."

Katie shakes her head and writes on a piece of paper: "Let the police do it."

"Nooo waaay. I caaan't."

Katie writes: "Look in the mirror."

I do and burst out laughing. These aren't normal facials. They're Fun Facials, slumber party specials courtesy of Katie's mom. My face is this bright fluorescent orange, and she looks like a cherry lollipop with hair.

"Yooour mooom isss meeentaaal!"

Katie giggles. Then she holds up her hand and shushes me while she stares at her watch for three minutes. Every time I go to say something, she kicks me.

"Oookaaay," she says at last. We wash our faces off, hers in the sink, mine in the bathtub. After we're done, we go back into the living room and I start up again.

"Leslie, come on," Katie says. "Calling those girls is the stupidest idea you've had in ages."

"Why? Don't you think they'd like to know they're not the only one? I bet they don't even know about each other—and they're in the same school!"

"You're such a busybody. Leave it alone."

"And it'll all go away?"

"I didn't say that."

"Katie, please. I'll only do it if you say it's okay. Puh-leeaasse? For meeeee?? Puh-llleeeeeaaaaasssse???"

Her eyes bug. "How does your mom put up with you?"

I give her a pretend hit on the arm, grab her hand and yank her into my bedroom. She sits on a pillow at the end of my bed. I call Information on my new cell phone, my heart doing loop-de-loops.

Luckily Port Burdock's not too big. Information has just five Bradys and two Benthams. I ask for all of them. Information's only allowed to give out three names per call, so I start with both Benthams and the first Brady.

I phone the first Bentham. A boy answers. There's the sound of a TV in the background. "Yeah?"

Even though he sounds little, I put on my polite voice. "Hello, this is Leslie Phillips. Could I please speak to Jill?"

The boy yells, "It's for you," and I hear this voice yell back, "I'll take it in my room." I've hit the jackpot, first try. The boy doesn't say anything else, but I can still hear the TV. Finally the other voice comes on the line.

"Hello?"

Oh my God. This is Jill Bentham, the girl in 9C. She must be in grade ten now. My grade. To think I know her phone number, where she lives, goes to school—what she looks like naked—and she doesn't even know I exist. I feel like I'm in an X-rated Nancy Drew book.

"Hello," I reply. It's all I get out.

"You can hang up." Jill says into the phone to her brother. Pause. I can still hear the TV. "I said, you can hang up now, Jeffrey!" I hear a click. "So, hi. Who is it?"

"Leslie Phillips. You don't know me, but I know you, sort of. At least, I know Jason McCready."

Her voice gets small. "Who did you say you were?"

"Leslie Phillips. I'm nobody. Just this girl. I went out with him."

I thought being humble, a kindred spirit or something, would make her friendly. Instead, she turns into *me* on a bad day. "Well, maybe you went out with him, but I didn't, and if you're the one who ratted my name to the police, I don't know how you know who I am, but you got me in trouble with my folks, so thank you very much, and don't ever call me again." She hangs up.

No way I'm giving up without a fight. "Katie," I say, "is it a sin to do something bad for a good cause?"

"I think so."

"Then say a prayer for me." I phone back. Jill answers. Before she can hang up on me again, I say quickly, "Look, I have the pictures, and if you don't talk to me I'm going to mail them to your dad, with a photocopy to the town newspaper."

"Oh God."

She sounds so scared, I'm ashamed to be blackmailing her. "What happened to you also happened to me," I say. "I want to charge him, but officially he's a first-time offender. If you charge him too, maybe we can put him away."

There's a pause. "Has anyone else seen the pictures?"

"No."

"Thank you. Thank you." She's practically kissing my feet over the phone line. "Promise me you won't show them ever. Not to anyone. Promise you'll burn them. Please?"

"Not till you agree to help me."

"But I can't!"

"Yes, you can."

"It's different for you," she says. Her voice is cracking. "He doesn't live here any more. I'm finally getting some sleep."

"No, you're not," I tell her. "He's in your head. He keeps waking you up."

"How do you know?"

"I just do." I hear her sob. I wish I could hug her.

"When that detective showed up at the door, I didn't know what it was all about." She blows her nose. "She got me alone in the living room and asked me all these questions: if I knew Jason, if he'd hurt me, if he'd raped me. I felt like a criminal. She said if I ever remembered anything to give her a call. After, she told my folks I hadn't done anything wrong, but they acted like they didn't believe her. Mom kept saying, 'We've never had trouble with the police.'"

Katie pantomimes like she wants to know what Jill's saying, but I give her a look and she settles down quick.

There's a catch in Jill's throat. "Look, it was the end of last year. I remember the flashing when he took the pictures. But not much else. I'd never had more than one glass of wine at Christmas dinner before that. I thought I was going to bleed to death. I tried to break up with him, but he wouldn't go away. Finally he went on that date with Jenny Maraida to make me jealous."

I get chills. "Who's Jenny Maraida?"

"You don't know? Her dad caught them drunk and naked in the family garage. He called the principal at the academy and Jason got booted out for what they called 'drunkenness and other grave misdemeanors.' If it was anybody but Dr. Maraida reporting him, nothing would have happened. I mean, the guys at the academy are rich kids in jackets and ties. They walk through town like they own the place."

"Back to Jason."

"No." Jill stops me cold. "I haven't seen him since. I never want to again. There must be somebody else who can help you."

"There is," I sigh. "A girl named Melanie Brady. I'll try her instead."

There's a weird pause. "You can't."

"Why not?"

"Melanie Brady is dead."

Forty

Melanie Brady committed suicide.

According to Jill, everyone came to school one day and there was this announcement that Melanie was dead. They never said how, but it got out that she took some pills and slit her wrists in the bathtub while her parents were out playing bridge.

Some people said it was because she used to get straight As and that year her marks were bad. She didn't have many friends, but everyone knew she was dating this guy from the academy, Jason. Things with him were supposed to be going really well.

School guidance counselors were busy all day dealing with weeping students who'd never talked to Melanie before. As Jill tells me this, I have a flash of Ashley. If I died, she'd be first in line to get attention. No, I take it back. When a person's dead, lots changes, and the rest doesn't matter.

The service at the funeral home was packed, Jill says. Jason was at the back, crying harder than anyone. A bunch of girls got indignant that he didn't get to sit with the family, seeing as he and Melanie'd been going steady for over a month. But her parents wouldn't even talk to him. In fact, when Jason went up to talk to them, Melanie's dad made a fist.

A kid who works part-time at the funeral home doing errands said he heard two of the undertakers talking about bruises on the body. That got lots of rumors going, the kind that go through high schools faster than flu. The stupidest was that Melanie didn't kill herself at all—the bruises were from falling in the bathtub and she drowned. Another was that the bruises came from her dad; everybody in town knew he was a mean drunk.

Jill says the kids liked the drowning rumor, because cutting your wrists is so awful. But the visitation was open casket and Melanie was in long sleeves. So that left the rumor about her dad.

"Forget the rumors," I say. "You know why she killed herself. We both do."

"So? We can't prove it. And even if we could, what good would it do? It won't bring her back. It won't do anything except make her parents feel bad." A long pause. "Please destroy the pictures?"

I feel a sudden wave of disgust, not at Jill but at myself for blackmailing her. "The pictures are history. I burned them ages ago."

"Oh God, thank you..." A deep breath. Look, about your trial. I wish I could help, but I can't. My dad's real conservative. Mom too. I'm supposed to be perfect. They'd die."

"Right," I say.

"Forgive me?"

"I don't know." And I hang up.

Katie gives me a back rub while I tell her about the call. Then we sit and stare out the window. We don't say anything. After a minute, Katie gets bored and idly starts to paint my toenails. I stop her before she puts Happy Faces on the big nails with Liquid Paper. She sighs and gets out her sparkle dust instead, like she's Martha Stewart on drugs or something.

"No, Katie. Not now!" I say sharply, and yank my foot away.

Katie sees my forehead scrunched up. "Sorry." She thinks I'm mad. But I'm not. I'm suddenly just very, very determined. "I know what I'm going to do."

"You've made the right decision," Katie says, as if she's read my mind. "It's too much, you getting grilled by his lawyers, and it all being for nothing."

"No, Katie. I'm not running away from it. I'm having Jason charged."

She gasps. "Are you serious?"

"No other girl will testify, so I know Jason will only get a slap on the wrist. But if I don't charge him, the next time he does it, he'll still be a 'first-time offender.' At least this way—me saying it out loud, in court, for everyone to hear—he won't be able to act innocent again. There'll be traces. Records. A history."

"What if he tries to get even?"

"He can come after me no matter what I do. Every time he's gotten away with things before, with Melanie or Jill or Beachball, he's gotten worse. The way I figure it, the only chance I have is to fight back."

"What if the judge doesn't believe you?"

"That's the least of my worries." And it really is. For a second, the truth of it makes me burst out laughing. Katie looks at me as if I've lost it. "I'm sick and tired of living in fear," I tell her. "I have to do something."

Katie says how much she admires me and how I'm either the bravest or the stupidest person she knows, or maybe both, but she's with me no matter what.

That night, Mom tells me the same thing, except she leaves out the "stupid" part.

Me, I'd leave the "brave" part out, too. It's like, after talking to Jill, I realized there's no choice. Not for me. Not for what I want to be, or see, when I look in the mirror.

Forty-one

After I tell Sylvia I'll testify, the police lay charges against Jason for rape, stalking, forcible confinement and uttering death threats. The same day, he's arrested and brought before a judge for what's called a detention hearing.

Jason gets bail, but there's a bunch of catches. He isn't allowed to contact me or to be anywhere near me. That means it's him who has to change schools. When he isn't at school, he has to stay on his family's property, too, and be inside by a six p.m. curfew. To make sure he obeys those rules, the judge makes his parents put up a ton of money as "security."

With Jason out of the picture, I go back to school again. Instead of running to the bathroom to cry all the time, I feel like I'm ten feet tall—I can take on the world. Who'd ever have guessed that going to school would make me feel so good?

It's especially fun watching Beachball suck up to me. Every time she sees me, she acts concerned and asks if there's anything she can do to help. (Like, for a start, go flush herself down the toilet?) My teachers give me extra breaks too. Guidance has obviously sent them confidential memos to take my "difficult situation" into consideration. Even Mr. Carrouthers has laid off.

Ms. James is ecstatic. The first time she saw me in the hall, she tried to give me a high five. Please. I backed off, but left her a little note in her staff mailbox saying thanks. The students are something else again. You'd think I was some sort of celebrity. Girls who used to ignore me come up to say that I'm amazing and should get an award or something. Right. They're basically looking for dirt. Meanwhile, guys make a point of steering clear, as if they think I'll charge them with harassment if they peek at my boobs.

Ernie Boulder was really funny. He came up all sweaty and smelly and said he hoped I knew that he was just kidding when he used to look up my skirt. "How interesting," I say, trying not to laugh. You should have seen him shake.

At last there's the preliminary hearing, where the judge hears if there's enough evidence to have a trial. Katie testifies that she saw my bruises and watched me burn the Polaroids. Dr. Seymour testifies as an expert on sexual assault.

But first, I take the stand. I swear an oath to tell the truth, and then I have to read some things from my journal and answer questions. I try to concentrate on what I'm being asked, but I can't help glancing at Jason. He's staring at me hard, smirking the whole time. Right behind him are his parents, dressed up, staring at me too, like I'm this psycho liar out to ruin their family.

Up against the McCreadys, I feel like trash. I almost lose control. But instead, I look at Mom. I don't want to let her down. I don't want to let myself down either. When I think about Jason's other victims, this mysterious power takes root inside me. It grows and grows, until every part of my body feels totally alive. I stop worrying. I face Jason, and, for a second, he looks away. Then I tell the truth. All of it.

The judge says the evidence is strong enough for Jason to stand trial.

The trial starts off like the preliminary hearing. Katie, Dr. Seymour and I testify like before.

Jason has a new lawyer, though, Mr. Addison. Addison's

an old guy with a silver mustache. He tries to trip me up, but I've come so far I'm not going to fall apart now. Instead, I pretend he's Carrouthers. People are a lot less scary when you focus on counting their nose hairs. Addison has better luck undermining Katie. He makes a big deal about how she's sworn a solemn oath on the Bible to tell the truth, and Katie gets so scared she ends up sounding uncertain. "You *think* that's what happened?" Addison asks sarcastically. "You don't know for sure?" Eventually, she starts to cry. Dr. Seymour does well, but Addison has a psychiatrist just as good on Jason's side, who says I'm a liar.

My lawyer, Mr. Pérez, isn't sure whether or not Addison will put Jason on the stand. But he does. Jason is slick. He says he can't apologize for what he hasn't done and he can't understand why I'm doing this; at the time, he thought I'd taken his breaking up with me pretty well.

Mr. Pérez doesn't let him off easy, but Jason holds his ground. He sits there acting earnest and sincere, like he actually believes what he's saying. He even has the nerve to slip me a wink as he leaves the stand.

But even Jason can't keep his cool when he gets the verdict: Guilty on all counts.

Forty-two

If I was making a movie, I'd have Jason sentenced to the pen for years and years, screaming for mercy as he's hauled away to a prison crawling with rats. I'd put him in a cell with a maniac who tortures him day and night the way he tortured me.

If I was a nicer person, I'd have him getting therapy and leaving prison a whole new person, seeking forgiveness and never doing another awful thing in his life. To be super cheesy, I'd maybe have him devote the rest of his life to charity.

But this isn't a story. It's the truth. And the truth isn't like that.

Jason's father doesn't show up for the sentencing hearing, but his mother is there, dressed in black and wearing shades. She's like a zombie. So is Jason. I'd imagined he'd at least be shaking, but he's so controlled it's frightening. When the judge asks if he has a statement to make before sentencing, he says, "Only one thing, Your Honor. I'm innocent."

When I hear that I start to get upset. But not for long. The judge adjusts his glasses, rips into him, talks about how he hopes Jason will reflect on his actions while in custody, and learn to take responsibility for his life. Then he passes sentence. Jason is taken away and it's all over.

Like Sylvia figured, he wasn't put away for long. Just eighteen months in Juvenile Detention. All the same, I'd do it over if I had to. Jason will never be a first-time offender again. Now he knows he can't always do whatever he wants and get away with it.

I'm still not sure what controls events. Is it destiny or fate? If there was a reason this stuff happened, I can't imagine what it would be. All I know is, I feel good about standing up for myself.

I've needed that kind of confidence since Jason got out. It's been six months now. He's in a military college out west, apparently. Dr. Seymour says I've probably seen the last of him. I'll never know for certain, but the fact he's moved away is a good sign. Also that he hasn't phoned. That doesn't stop me thinking, though. Especially about the poor girl out there somewhere who's in love with him. I wish her luck.

Writing in my journal has helped. In fact, Dr. Seymour says it's therapeutic. One of these days, I should probably get in touch with Ms. Graham. She's taken early retirement. I'll bet she'd like to know that she made a difference in someone's life. After all, without her, I wouldn't have had a journal, and the evidence would have been just my word against Jason's. Like Katie says, sometimes good things come from unexpected places.

Who knows? I look in the faces of all the new grade nines and tens. Some of them have Jasons, but they don't let on. When they hear my story through the grapevine, they'll know they're not alone. But what about all the other girls in the same situation? I close my eyes and try to send them strength. Katie calls it praying. I call it mental telepathy. Either way, I figure it can't hurt.

Still, with what I've been through, there's got to be a bigger way to shake things up. I'll start by talking to Katie. Between the two of us, we'll figure out something.

A Note on the Law

The legal terminology used in this book is drawn from American law. In Canada, the correct legal term for rape is sexual assault; the correct legal term for stalking is criminal harassment.

If you've enjoyed this novel from Annick Press, check your local bookstore or favorite on-line retailer for *Double or Nothing* by Dennis Foon. This powerful story about a teenage boy who is relentlessly drawn into the world of gambling has been described as "...a novel that crackles with life."

Check out our Web site at www.annickpress.com for further information on this title, as well as purchasing information.

From *Double or Nothing...*

CHAPTER ONE

This classroom smells moldy, just like this whole school. Mold oozes from the walls. The teachers plaster their rooms with posters of dead writers and extinct animals to hide it, to no avail. The building's not that old, but the mold set in about fifteen seconds after they cut the ribbon and opened the doors. It's a scientific phenomenon. Schools make mold.

Those spores don't get on me, though. That fine green dust that covers people the instant they sit down, that turns them into nodding zombies, Teflons right off me. I'm immune because I'm awake. I'm awake because my life has spice. What's the spice? No big secret, really. Let me explain.

When some people sit, they just sit. No wonder they're bored. No wonder life seems like a never-ending story. Let's say we're sitting in the cafeteria, twiddling our thumbs or pushing slop back and forth across the plate. That is boredom. But say I add some spice. I bet you five bucks that the next person to walk through the door will be a girl. Some might say, screw you, I'm not risking my hard-earned cash, and go back to sliding the slop. But a wise person would reply, you're on, and all of a sudden, we're staring at that door. Like that portal becomes pure mystery and excitement. Who will walk through next? Boy or girl? Who will get the money? This is the buzz. This is the thing that brings the spark, a flame, some pleasure, to the otherwise dull, useless, boring thing some people call life.

My pal Bongo understands this. Bongo might look like a Guinea Pig, and his brainpower might be in the GP's arena, but he's a player. A loser, but a player. And, hey, I don't begrudge that at all. At least he plays. At least he's into shaking it up. He turns to me in English class. We're both dying. The crabtooth, Mr. Cheese, a.k.a. Belch Face, a.k.a. Fart Machine, a.k.a. Most Boring Human Turd on Earth, is droning on about Hamlet.

Now, I got nothing against Hamlet. He was cool. He saw ghosts and had duels and was a kill-or-be-killed kind of guy. I mean, Mel Gibson played him between *Lethal Weapon 1* and *Lethal Weapon 2*, so this play can't be all bad. But my teacher, the Human Cheese, he's murdering Shakespeare. Each word that dribbles out of his mouth is pure somnambulism, and people are dropping like flies. I'm not kidding. Every couple of minutes you hear a thud as somebody's head hits their desk, dead asleep. Mr. Cheese doesn't care, he's just babbling on and on. He takes the snoring as some kind of affirmation.

That's when Bongo turns to me and says, "Hey, Kip, I'm dying here, man." He's pale, Cheese has vampirized his life force — and something has got to be done.

I smile. "It's resurrection time, pal."

The tension on Bongo's face melts in pure relief. "You're the man, Kip, you're the man. What's the bet?" Bongo's so filled with anticipation, I can see a little drool forming at the corner of his mouth.

"I say the Cheese does a belch in the next twenty seconds."

Bongo grins. "Five bucks he doesn't."

I shake my head. Once a GP, always a GP. Here we are, being turned into granite by the dullest human being on earth, and Bongo proposes a five-dollar wager. I almost fall asleep at the proposal, it's so pathetic. But I try to remain respectful.

"No buzz in that. Ten."

Bongo then has the reflex reaction of the weak: he feels his wallet. Not like he opens it, just pats it, reminding himself of the contents or lack thereof. A worried look crosses his face as he mulls over the odds of beating me (slim to none) versus how much coin he requires to get through the week. I shrug.

"No problem, Bong, forget it. Go back to the land of the dead."

Bongo bristles at the insinuation that he is faint-hearted. He pulls out his wallet and lifts the secret flap that hides his special stash. Produces a ten-spot.

"I'm in."

Now we are happy. Now we have a reason to live. We both pull out our watches, push the little buttons that set up the stopwatch function, and Bongo counts down.

"Three, two, one—Go!" Bongo whispers, and we click simultaneously. Mr. Cheese, mopping his forehead with his handkerchief, babbles on.

"But when Hamlet pulls back the drapery to reveal the dead Polonius, he has little idea . . . "

Bongo leans in on me, hissing: "Fourteen, thirteen . . . "

". . . of the terrible repercussions his bloody act will unleash," the Cheese continues. "So much destruction from one death, the death of an old, irrelevant man . . . "

Bongo's getting excited: time's running out for me. Me, I'm hearing what Cheese is saying for the first time. The educational power of a bet is extraordinary.

"Ten, nine, eight . . . " Bongo's grinning.

But I'm not worried, no fret here, because something amazing is happening. Ten seconds ago I was bored to tears, nodding off, half-dead from watching the most tedious person on the planet kill me with words. But now, miraculously, I'm watching a human being transform before my eyes. I'm an eyewitness to an incredible metamorphosis. Suddenly, Mr. Cheese is riveting.

At least for us, because THUNK. Another kid's head hits his desk. They're still with the *old* Mr. Cheese. For them, time and space haven't been reconfigured. For them, there is no spice.

Bongo, thrilled, goes on with the countdown: "Five, four . . . "

Will he, won't he, will he, won't he? Bongo, feeling his chops, touches his wallet, imagining the dollars he's about to win. Bad move.

Through it all, Mr. Cheese is oblivious. "But in Hamlet's world, the fragile chain of life is broken, and the life-links . . . "

Bongo is feeling triumphant. To him it's in the bag. He's already deciding on how to spend it. On burgers? A new CD?

He's chortling: "Three, two . . . "

Mr. Cheese: " . . . drop like . . . "

But wait! Mr. Cheese pauses. Feels something. And from deep in his intestines, invisible gases rise, rise, rise, and . . . he belches. Unmistakably.

" . . . flies."

Mr. Cheese wipes his sweaty forehead again. Most of the class is snoring, so they don't smell the delicious perfume of sausage and pickles. Bongo does. He's wilted like a crushed daisy. Feeling sorry for the poor guy, I generously offer him a way out of the blues — and a bit more excitement for us both. After all, there's still another fifteen minutes left in the Cheese Show.

"C'mon, Bongo, double or nothing," I benevolently offer.

"I don't got it."

I look at his sorrowful face and, filled with empathy for his condition, I try to make him see the light.

But I know he's buckling, he always does. What makes Bongo a loser? Why can't he escape the mold? Because he panics, he gets worried. He stops having fun. And that's what it's about, right? Fun.

"Think, Bongo: win and we're square."

Bongo, defeated, shakes his sorry, furry head.

"Lose and I'm down twenty. I fold."

Sullen, Bongo hands me a ten-dollar bill, which I press against my nose. It smells good.